D1458513

The Film Star's Dark Secret

Copyright 2016 Nick Shaw
Published by Nick Shaw at Kindle Direct Publishing

License Notes
This book is an original story by the author.

ISBN: 978-1-5209-8649-4

Table of Contents

Prologue
Missy – Nashville 2004

"Have you flown from LA to offer me just a role in an interracial porn movie?"

Missy was upset. When Jake Bronstein, her agent, told her that he was flying to meet her in Nashville, she thought that he was negotiating a deal for a television series.

"Alberto Massimo is one of the leading Italian film directors acclaimed for his films. You simply cannot pass up this chance."

Don, bald and bespectacled, had a twitch in his right eye. Today it was worse, which meant that he was nervous. Dressed in just a coloured Hawaii shirt and white cotton trousers, Don was also probably freezing in her air-conditioned home office. She pretended not to notice his discomfort.

"Don, I've never worked with any of those fancy foreign film directors. Their so-called art films usually fail at the box office."

Missy was being provocative. Actually, she liked the idea of doing an art film. Presently she had the image of a vintage blonde sex icon. However, she had never worked with a foreign film director and was unsure about her acting talents.

"Alberto's art films have won rave reviews. This is the first time that he is doing a film in North America, working with American actors."

Missy had a long relationship with Jake. She trusted him. During the heydays of the studios, he got her good contracts. Now the studios were gone and Jake had no choice but to negotiate with independent producers.

"Where will the film be shot?"

Missy was hoping that it would be at Columbia or MGM. It would be like the old times.

"Don Prince, the producer, wants to shoot the film in Toronto. The city offers subsidies to film makers."

"First, you want me to perform with a black actor. Now you are saying that I will have to spend a couple of weeks in Toronto to shoot the film. Do you have any other bad news?"

2

"Please consider yourself lucky to be offered a role with Richard Collins. He is still good-looking for his age."

"I've heard of him. Didn't he act as a Harlem detective in the black exploitation films of the seventies?"

"Yeah, he was quite a hit in those days. He even had a few brief love scenes with white starlets in some of his films. It was quite daring for that era."

"Starlets wanting a break into movies are willing to do anything."

"Look, Missy. There were movies like 'Hundred Rifles' with Raquel Welch and Jim Brown from the seventies that did well on the box office. It didn't harm Raquel's career."

"That's one example only."

"There are others. Stella Stevens had a hot love scene with Jim Brown in 'Slaughter'. They were in bed and she was kissing him. It was almost like soft porn and it was also in the seventies. She is from Alabama and it went with the audiences."

"Are you suggesting that I do a soft porn movie in the same style with Richard Collins?"

"Yes and the only difference is that Alberto will be directing the film. This will be an art film for sophisticated European audiences. It might even be presented at the Cannes film possibilities. Please think about the possibilities."

"Alright, Don. Give me a day to mull over it and I'll get back to you."

Missy was tempted but apprehensive that doing a film with a black man might rake up some skeletons in her cupboard from the past.

Chapter 1
Missy – Los Angeles 1962

"You look pretty enough to work as a model for us but we don't hire anybody younger than eighteen."

The man sitting behind the reception desk looked interested. Although fortyish, he sported an Elvis Presley type pompadour hairstyle and an embroidered white shirt. She could not see more because there was just a dim light in the black-walled room.

"I've just passed my eighteenth birthday two months ago," Missy replied.

She opened her bag and took out her driver's licence. The man studied it and handed it back to her.

"By the way, my name is Barry Dexter. Call me Barry."

"Your ad in the newspaper mentioned that you were hiring models for glamour photography. I thought that this could be a job opportunity for me."

"Do you know what this job requires?" Barry sat back and his chair creaked in protest.

"No. I think a photo model is somebody who models for pin-up pictures like Bettie Page."

"Well, our kind of photo modelling is a little different. Our models pose for customers who book sessions for taking photos in our studio."

"Is this a regular job with a salary?"

"Sure, you will work in shifts with regular breaks in between."

"Are there any special requirements?"

"Yes." Barry studied her face for a few seconds. "You'll have to pose topless and sometimes in the nude."

"I'm not so sure that I am ready for nude shots. I've never done this before."

"Well, it depends on how badly you want this job."

"I won a prize in a Nashville beauty contest and a Hollywood talent scout offered me a free trip to Los Angeles. I did a screen test and am waiting for a call from the studio."

"Listen, Los Angeles is crawling with young girls like you looking for an opportunity to act in a film. Most of the models in my studio are trying to make it in Hollywood. They are working here till they find something better."

"What do your models do?"

"They pose on a couch for a customer to take photos on a one-to-one basis. The sessions can last from fifteen minutes to an hour."

"What about the pay?"

"We pay on a weekly basis for a forty-hour week. There will be four-hour shifts and we will plan your shift schedule. The pay will be three hundred dollars a week."

Missy did a quick calculation. She was running out of money and her motel bill was up due for payment.

"I can give it a try for a week."

Barry smiled.

"I'll need to check you out. Make sure that your body is as good as your face."

"You want me to strip?"

"We've a dressing room where the models change. Are you ready?"

Without waiting for an answer, Barry stood up and walked from behind the reception desk.

"I guess there's a first time for everything."

"You bet," Barry said, leading the way to a corridor with four doors.

"Those two doors lead to our studios." Barry pointed to the two doors on the right side of the corridor. "Right now they are occupied."

He knocked on a door on the left side and then opened it.

"This is the dressing room for our models."

Missy followed Barry into a large room with lockers on one side and a long dressing table and mirror on the other side.

"You can strip here," Barry said, closing the door.

Missy hesitated, wondering whether she should follow his instructions or just back out at this moment.

"Please hurry. I do not have the whole day. There is nobody at the desk."

Missy unbuttoned her blouse and took it off.

"Take off your bra," Barry commanded.

She unhooked her brassiere to expose her breasts.

"Nice tits." Barry had an appreciative look.

Missy knew that her 36C size breasts with their light pink aureoles were just right for glamour photography.

"How about taking off the rest?" Barry sounded impatient.

Missy took off her belt and unbuttoned her skirt. Letting it drop to her feet, she picked it up and placed it on one of the dressing table stools.

She hesitated for a moment before placing her thumbs under the elastic of her panties and pulling them down up to her ankles. Wobbling unsteadily on her high heels, she stepped out of her panties from one shoe but tangled with the other. Barry had an amused look while she picked up her panties from the heel of her shoe and flung them on the stool.

Now she was naked and feeling vulnerable in front of this male who was scrutinizing her body as if it was a piece of meat. Instinctively she placed her right hand in front of her crotch.

"No tattoos, no skin blemishes, no operation scars. You're almost perfect for the job."

"Thank you. May I put on my clothes now?"

"Yes. May I suggest that you trim your bush a little?" Barry pointed to her crotch.

Missy felt embarrassed. Being a natural blonde-haired person, she just had a light-coloured patch of pubic hair. It was just fluff and she never thought it as unruly. She decided to clip it a little.

"OK, I'll leave you to dress. Please see me at the reception to sign a contract." Barry turned away and left.

When she had just finished dressing, she heard a knock and the door opened. A redhead in a bathing robe entered the room.

"I'm sorry but I didn't think that there would be anybody in the dressing room," she apologized.

"Hi, my name is Rosemary and I've just finished my shift. Are you the new girl?"

Missy saw that she had a slight sheen on her face as they shook hands.

"My name is Missy McGuire and Barry has just hired me."

The two women talked about their origins and Rosemary explained that she was from Minnesota and had been in Los Angeles since two years.

"I tried to get into the movies but had a lousy agent. Now I am doing freelance work as a pin-up model and a couple of shifts here. It is something temporary until something better turns up."

Rosemary opened a locker and took off her bathrobe. She did not seem to be concerned about being nude in front of a stranger while she looked into her locker. Missy noticed that she had a lush body with heavy breasts and a slight bulge at the stomach. The clipped bush on her crotch was barely noticeable.

"What's the work like here?" Missy asked, hoping that Rosemary would tell about the pitfalls.

"Well, it is a little boring when compared to doing pin-up shots. The room has a couch where you lie either topless or in the nude. Since it is a photo studio, the customers are obliged to have cameras. They tell you how to pose and take shots of you."

"Isn't it a bit risky? I mean strangers taking pictures and then circulating them around to friends?"

"Well, the men who come have to be members of the studio and sign an agreement that the photos are for private use only."

"Do these men make any special requests for poses?"

"Some men may ask you to give a seductive smile. Others may ask you to strip nude and spread your legs." Rosemary had put on a black brassiere and was pulling up a pair of black panties.

"Do you have to agree to such requests?"

"It depends. I have regulars who I do oblige. Most are lonely old men looking for a chat with a woman."

"They could go to a bar if they wanted to pick up a woman."

"No, these are shy types. They probably jack off on the pictures that they have taken."

Missy was shocked at Rosemary's language but the woman seemed cynical about her work. She had put on a white blouse and was pulling her jeans up over her broad hips.

"This is the first time I'm doing something like this and I'm a little uncomfortable."

"Don't worry, baby. There is a first time for everything. You'll soon get used to it."

"What happens if any of the men get aggressive?"

"Nobody will touch you. That's against the rules." Rosemary sat down on a stool facing the dressing table mirror and beckoned to Missy to sit beside her.

"It's hot in there under the klieg lights. That is the tough part of this job." She dabbed her face with a tissue.

"What happens if a man does touch you?"

"There's a red button beside the couch and Barry will be there in a New York second."

"Has it ever happened to you?"

"No. I do cases of men touching themselves but ignore it unless they pull it out. When I warn them, they usually stop. We can't have cum all over the floor."

Rosemary talked casually as she applied fresh lipstick on her lips.

"Is there anything else that I need to know?"

"Some of the men come with cameras without film. They ask for special poses, take a good look and then click the camera button but I can make out that they are not taking any shots."

"Why would they do that?"

"They probably bought an old camera in a flea market just to get into the studio. They don't have the money to buy film or develop photos."

"You mean they just come to look?"

"Well, they get their kicks by making us pose for them. It's a little more expensive than going to a strip bar but they get to have a close look at a nude woman."

Rosemary got up and returned to take her handbag from her locker.

"I've got to rush. Talk to you another time." She gave Missy a brief peck on her cheek and left the room.

Missy decided that she would take the job. She badly needed the money.

Chapter 2
Missy – Los Angeles 1962

"Can you move your legs a little apart?"

Missy had assumed a seductive pose for black man with a camera in his hand. She had already taken off her panties at the man's request. Now she was on the couch with her hands behind her head and her knees up. It was a frequent request from her customers.

"Sure," she said, moving her knees just a little apart so that the man could get a view of her crotch.

She took a tissue to wipe her face. It was hot as the man moved the klieg light closer towards her.

"That is nice." The man moved to the foot of the couch and bent forward to look. He did not take any photographs. By now, Missy knew that some men came just to have a look at her nude body. She had now been working for a fortnight at the photo studio and gotten used to its tawdry atmosphere.

"You've have a beautiful body." The man was still staring at her pudenda. Turned on by his look of admiration, she felt blood rushing to her mound. She opened her legs wider to expose her inner labia.

"That's wonderful." The man seemed mesmerized by the sight of her intimate parts.

The man's look of concentration was briefly disturbed when the room air-conditioner noisily sprang into operation. There was a constant hum but Missy, although nude, welcomed the cool air.

Missy noticed that she had been getting a large proportion of black men requesting one-to-one sessions with her. Probably the word had got around among black men that there a blonde beauty in the studio. At first, she had been uncomfortable but most of them just wanted to see a naked white woman.

She noticed the man get up and walk around the couch. He was young with short curly hair and a slim moustache. Now he was looking down on her.

"How would you like to make some good money?" He had a sinister smile.

"What do you mean?"

"I mean we could meet outside when you're free."

"I'm sorry but I'm a photo model and we do not fraternize with customers."

"I'll make it worth your while."

"I don't understand."

"I'm willing to pay two hundred dollars for a one-hour sex session with you. It can be either at your place or my pad."

Missy was surprised that the man was willing to offer so much money. Although he was neatly dressed in a checked shirt and cotton trousers, he did not have the look of a big spender.

"I'm afraid but it's out of question."

"Please don't say no. The other girls do it."

Missy was surprised. Rosemary was not the type who would engage in sex for money. She did not know the other girls so well. Perhaps the man was bluffing.

"I don't believe you. Please let us stop this conversation."

"Have it your way." The man shrugged his shoulders.

"Please, if you don't mind."

"My offer still holds in case I come past the next time."

He smiled and left the room.

Missy was shocked and surprised. She was shocked at the audacity of the black man offering money to have sex with her. At the same time, she was surprised at the amount of money he had proposed. It amounted to almost a week of work at the studio.

When her shift was over, she decided to talk to Barry about the conversation. Fortunately, Barry was alone reading the sports paper.

"Can I ask you a question?"

"Sure." Barry looked up from his paper.

"A man propositioned me during a photo session."

"What kind of proposition was it?" Barry did not seem overly curious.

"He offered me money to meet him outside."

"What you do in your own time does not concern me." Barry went back to reading his newspaper.

"He wanted to have sex with me."

"Look, I am there to protect you. You press the button in case you are uncomfortable with the man's behaviour. Otherwise, it is between you and the man."

"My last client was black."

Barry looked up his paper.

"You've to be careful. Some of these black men are pimps looking for white women for their stables."

"This man was young and seemed nice."

"It could be that he had the money and the itch." Barry laughed.

"What you're saying is that you don't care if we meet clients outside working hours?"

"You're a big girl and have to decide for yourself. Ask the other girls."

Missy decided to ask Rosemary for her advice how to handle such situations.

* * * * *

A few days later Missy bumped into Rosemary in the locker room. Rosemary was late and was undressing in a hurry.

Missy explained how the black man had offered her money for sex.

"Do you get such proposals?" Missy asked.

"Yes but I turn them down. You never know with the weird kind of men who come to the studio."

"This man was offering two hundred dollars. That's a lot of money."

Rosemary raised her eyebrow just as she put on her bathrobe. "You were actually considering taking him up on his offer?"

"No," Missy protested. "I'm just telling you about it." Actually, she could have used the money.

"Why don't you check with Rhonda?"

"I haven't met her yet. How does she look?"

"She is a peroxide blonde with a big butt. She does a few tricks on the side. Some of her johns are coloured men."

"I've got to rush." Rosemary brushed Missy's cheek with her lips and left the locker room.

Missy decided not to check with Rhonda. Beneath the surface, Hollywood was about sex and money. She had to make her choice.

* * * * *

"Your next appointment is with Eddie Conklin," Barry announced as Missy reported for work.

"Will it be the usual fifteen minute session?"

"No, Eddie does some glamour photography on the side and is always looking out for new models. He has asked for a thirty-minute session."

"Does he have any special requests?"

"He'll probably want some artistic nude shots. You'll have to do a bit of posing."

Missy left for the dressing room, hoping that she would get a break as a photo model.

When Eddie entered the photo room, she was surprised to see a big, brown-skinned man in a white T-shirt and jeans with two cameras and a tripod stand. This was not one of her usual customers.

"Hi, I'm Edward Conklin. Just call me Eddie." Missy felt her body blush as he sized her up from head to toe. The man looked fiftyish, had carefully coiffed curly greying hair, light-colored eyes and a moustache. He was upscale compared to her usual customers.

"I'm Missy."

"That's a nice name. Are you from the South?"

"I'm from Nashville."

"How long have you been in LA?"

"I've been here for just about a month."

They talked a bit. Eddie did not seem to be in a hurry to take any photographs.

"I've heard that you do glamour photography," Missy said. Eddie had been asking too many questions about her personal life and she wanted him to stop talking and take some photographs.

"I do some photography but that's not my main line of business."

Missy was disappointed but not surprised. It was rare for a colored male to be photographing white female models.

12

"What kind of business?"

"I'm a talent agent."

"Do you represent artistes and performers?"

Eddie smiled slyly.

"Well, all sorts of people. I also have contracts with a few boxers and set up fights for them."

"I don't know much about boxing," Missy admitted.

"Ever heard of Jackson Coots?" Eddie mounted a Rolleiflex camera on his tripod.

"No."

"I'm setting up fights so that he becomes the welterweight champion."

Missy did not comment while Eddie talked about how he first met Jackson Coots in a Bronx gym. All the while, he was looking in his camera to take a shot.

"Let's change the subject," Eddie suggested. "I'll be taking a face and shoulders shot of you."

Missy was surprised. Most men wanted to take nude shots of her. Perhaps Eddie was into glamour photography.

"Look at the camera but you don't need to smile."

Missy followed his instructions as he took of her face and its profile.

"Now I want you to just lie with your hands on your sides and your legs together."

Eddie took a couple of photos.

"Now I need one last photo with you sitting up with your knees folded under you and your hand on your crotch."

It took a while for Missy to assume the pose that Eddie wanted but she finally managed it.

"That's fine. I'm done." Eddie started to unmount the camera from the tripod.

"By the way, are you happy with the money that you're making on this job?"

"Actually I'm hoping to break into movies. This is just a temporary thing."

Eddie nodded as if he understood her situation.

"I know but are you satisfied with your wages?"

"I' always like to make more. Everyone does."

Eddie took out a visiting card from his shirt top pocket.

"Here's my card. Give me a call in case you want an opportunity to make a few extra bucks."

Missy looked at the card. There was Eddie's name and a telephone number.

"Don't you have an office?"

"Like I said, I'm a talent agent. My office is where the talent is." Eddie winked and gave a big smile.

"What kind of work do you have in mind?"

"I'm thinking of some sort of escort work."

Eddie looked at her while folding his tripod.

"You know there are lonely men out there who would appreciate the company of a classy blonde like you."

"Does it involve sex?"

"It may or may not. The money will be good. I'll be your agent."

Missy thought that he would be more like a pimp than an agent.

"Think about it." Eddie looked at his watch. "I've got to go. Feel free to give me a call whenever you feel like it."

Eddie's mysterious offer and his easy-going manner intrigued Missy. He certainly did not look like one of those flashy pimps in fur coats and gold chains.

* * * * *

At the end of her shift, Missy asked Barry about Eddie.

"Eddie told me that he is a talent agent. What does he do?"

"I really don't know. They say that he has connections with boxing promoters and the Mafia."

"He seems to be some sort of photographer with two fancy cameras. Do you think that he is a freelance glamour photographer?"

Barry smirked.

"I've never seen his name in any glamour magazines. May he has a private collection of nude photos."

Missy left with a feeling that she would cross paths with Eddie.

Chapter 3
Missy – Las Vegas 1963

"You want to try your luck again?"

Missy was at the roulette table at the Golden Nugget in Las Vegas and had just won a pile of red chips after placing a straight bet on seven, her favorite number. Her first impulse was to leave the table and cash in on her chips.

A barmaid came past with a tray of drinks. Missy took a martini and gulped it. The alcohol first burned her throat and then left her with a heady feeling.

"You can try an outside bet. The pay-out will be smaller but your chances will be better," the croupier helpfully suggested. She was a smart-looking black-haired young woman wearing a red bowtie and red jacket on a long-sleeved white blouse.

"I'm not so sure about those kinds of bets," Missy said. Although there were a number of other players around the table, waiting to place their next bets, the croupier explained the different types of bets and recommended that she bet on either a color or a number.

"Do you want to bet on red or black?"

"How do I bet on a number?"

"You can bet on the number being even or odd."

Missy thought about her favorite numbers, mainly odd like three, seven and nine. One part of her wanted to leave. On the other hand, she had taken up the croupier's time and the other people around the table were waiting to place their bets. The martini had boosted her self-confidence.

"I'll bet on an odd number," Missy announced, moving all her chips towards the croupier.

"Odd number," the croupier repeated.

When the other people finished placing their bets, the croupier spun the wheel in one direction and the white ball in the other direction. The ball spun at a high speed around the tilted circular track on the circumference of the wheel. Missy watched in fascination as it lost its momentum and slowed down.

"Please drop in an odd number pocket," she silently prayed.

The ball fell down into the wheel and dropped into the pocket with the number ten. In a quick motion, the croupier raked away her pile of red chips. It took a few seconds for Missy to realize that she had lost everything.

The croupier had lost interest in her and she moved away from the roulette table. On the way to the restroom, she picked up another martini from the barmaid walking around with complimentary drinks. She needed the drink to relieve her sense of anxiety.

Coming out of the restroom, she heard a familiar voice.

"Hey, fancy meeting you here." She saw Eddie Conklin. He was dressed in a black bowtie and tuxedo.

"Hello, Eddie." They shook hands.

"What brings you to Las Vegas?"

"I had this special weekend promotional offer with a free bus ride from LA to Las Vegas." Missy wondered why she was telling him about her cut-rate weekend outing.

"Are you staying at the Golden Nugget?"

"Yes, they had a special rate with the promotion."

"Good for you. You deserve a break from that studio job."

"Do you come often to Las Vegas?"

"I'm here on a business trip to negotiate a deal on behalf of one of my boxers."

"Why kind of deal are you negotiating?"

"Let's go to the bar for a drink and I'll tell you all about it."

She felt Eddie's arm on her elbow as he guided her to the bar. After asking her what she wanted to drink, he ordered two martinis.

"We are scheduling a fight for Jackson Coots, one of my fighters, in Las Vegas next month."

"I'm afraid but I am not much into boxing," Missy admitted.

"Well, we're planning a warm-up fight for Jackson in Las Vegas. If he wins, the next one will be in Madison Square Garden in New York."

"I didn't know that you were into big time boxing."

"Jackson will be the next world welterweight champion. Would like to meet him?"

Missy was feeling lightheaded with the martinis going to her head.

16

"I've just lost a pile of money at the roulette table and thinking of going to bed."

"I could make it worth your while." Eddie smiled and touched her arm.

"I don't understand."

"I want to give Jackson a surprise. He is from Harlem and never been with a white woman."

"Are you suggesting that I spend some time with him?"

"I'd like you to take care of him, like have sex with him."

"Eddie, I'm not kind of girl. I might pose nude for photos but I don't have sex with strangers."

"I'll make it worth your while."

"What do you mean?"

"I'll pay you a thousand dollars in cash if you allow Jackson to spend some time with you in your room."

Missy swallowed. Eddie's offer surprised her. It was a lot of money and she could use it.

"Why are you making me this offer? I'm sure that there are lots of escorts in Vegas who would be willing to oblige for less money."

"Listen, Missy, you've got class. I know that Jackson will fall for your type."

"Do you honestly think that I'm a hooker?"

"Not exactly but there is a first time for everything."

"Tell me, Eddie, are you a pimp?"

"Hey, I just want Jackson to have a good time. He has been working out hard and there will be no sex for him before the bout."

"Frankly, I could use the money in my present situation."

"Do I take it that you accept my proposal?" Eddie gave her an intense look.

"What do I have to do?"

"I just want you to say hello to Jackson. If you agree to meet up with him, I'll slip him a note with your room number. He will leave us and knock on your door half-an-hour later."

"I take it that you want me to have sex with him?"

"Yes and I'll pay you upfront when we part company."

Eddie patted his right trouser pocket.

"I'm quite nervous."

"Have another martini. It will relax you." Eddie beckoned to the barman, pressing a few bills in his hand.

"I'll look for a house phone to give Jackson a call." Eddie left, giving her a reassuring smile.

Missy downed her Martini. After the usual burning sensation in her throat, she felt warmth spread in her chest. She hoped that the alcohol would help in lowering her inhibitions.

By the time Eddie came back, she was feeling light-headed.

"It's better that we meet Jackson outside the hotel," Eddie suggested.

They walked towards the entrance.

"Two years ago, coloured people were not even allowed in this casino," Eddie explained. "We've to be careful. People will recognize Jackson and they won't like it if he is seen talking with a white woman."

Once they were outside, they walked to the one side of the hotel entrance, away from the hall porters. Soon a tall black man joined them. He had short curly hair, a broad nose and a scar on his cheek. His height and bulk gave him an intimidating look.

"Missy, this is Jackson," Eddie said. They shook hands.

"I'm pleased to meet you. Eddie told me a lot about you," Jackson said. Missy was surprised at the voice. Although it had a strong Bronx accent, it was soft-spoken for a man of his hulk.

"Jackson would like you know you better. Are you game?"

Missy decided to go for it.

"Yes."

"Can he meet you in your room?"

"I'm in room 430."

"Fine, he will be there in thirty minutes." Eddie scribbled the number on the back of his visiting card and handed it to Jackson. He patted Jackson on his shoulder.

"I'll be there," Jackson said, briskly turning around before leaving the two alone.

Eddie reached into his pocket and pulled out his billfold.

"Here is your one grand," he said, as he handed ten one-hundred dollar bills to Missy.

Missy took the money, stuffing it in her purse.

"Thanks, Eddie."

"Take good care of my boy," Eddie said. "I'll just take a walk along the Strip." He turned away and left.

"I've become a pro," Missy thought. She made up her mind to give Jackson a good time.

Chapter 4
Missy – Las Vegas 1963

Back in her room, Missy went to the bathroom and drank a glass of water. After all those martinis, she needed to clear her head. Still a little tipsy, she lay on her bed.

Hearing the telephone ring, she reached out to the bedside table. It took her a while to pick up the receiver.

"Hi, this is Jackson." She recognized the voice immediately.

"Hello." Missy started shaking, wondering why he was calling.

"I'll knock thrice on the door so that you will know that it is me. Will it be okay if I come in twenty minutes?"

"That will be fine. I'll be expecting you."

"Thanks." Jackson hung up.

Missy decided to freshen up for the occasion. She took a quick shower and then dabbed generous amounts of her favourite Max Factor Primitif perfume around her face and neck. Looking through her cupboard, she wished that she had thought of bringing a garter belt and pair of stockings. The only sexy apparel she found was her pink nightie set and she decided to wear it.

As she was putting on her black high heels, she heard the three knocks. She opened the door immediately to see Jackson staring at her in a star-struck manner. Letting him in, she realized that he was just as nervous as she was.

"Let's sit for a while," she suggested. He followed her to the round table with two chairs in the corner of the room. Jackson was clearly deferential as he took his place. She felt assured.

"I've never done this before," she admitted.

"I take it that this is your first time with a coloured man?"

Missy was relieved that he had misunderstood her. They were now talking about race, not sex for money.

"Yes." It was the truth.

"If you want to know, this is my first time with a white woman," Jackson said, looking down at the floor.

Suddenly Missy felt assured. Despite his hulk, Jackson seemed respectful towards her.

"Why don't we just talk a bit," Missy suggested. "Tell me something about yourself."

Jackson was silent, as if he did not know where to begin.

"Where were you born?" Missy asked helpfully.

"I was born in Harlem but my family moved to the Bronx when I was a child."

Missy followed up with a number of questions until Jackson opened up and started talking about how he started boxing with his father as his mentor. He mentioned how Eddie had approached his father after he had won a few amateur bouts,. Eddie had assured his father that he had good connections in the boxing world and could get him started as a professional fighter.

"How is it working out?" Missy was eager to know more about Eddie.

"Eddie set me up for a couple of bouts, mainly short fights before the main events in cities like Boston and Chicago. The money was not bad."

"What about the upcoming fight in Vegas?"

"This will be a big one. I am fighting Lee Hanson, a white boxer, and the winner gets to fight Emile Griffith for the WBC welterweight championship." Jackson sounded excited.

"How do you feel about your fight with Hanson?"

"I'm confident and in good shape. It took a while for Eddie to set up the fight."

"I think that Eddie and you make a good team."

"Eddie has contacts with the mob and they decide which fights will take place in Las Vegas. This will be a big one."

They talked for a while about the upcoming fight and Jackson's earlier shyness gave way to an infectious enthusiasm. Missy felt that this was the right time to get started.

"Would you like to kiss me?"

Jackson seemed confused for a moment and then laughed nervously. Missy decided to take the initiative. She got up, went over to him and then boldly sat on his lap.

"I do hope that I am not too heavy."

"You're light as a feather." Jackson fidgeted so that both his legs carried her weight.

She caressed Jackson's cheek with the back of her right hand.

"You're a flatterer." They laughed.

21

She put her hand behind his neck and pulled him towards her. Leaning in for a kiss, she pressed her lips against his. It was a long kiss and she felt Jackson's breathing quicken.

"That was good," she said when they broke contact.

"It was good for me too," Jackson said.

The next time they kissed, Missy probed her tongue into Jackson's mouth. It was a deep kiss. She shifted her position on his lap towards his crotch and felt his erection against her right hip.

"Let's get more comfortable. Why don't you take off all your clothes and join me in bed?"

She got off Jackson's lap and stood over him. He stood up too, uncertain what to do next.

Missy helped him take off his coat and then went to the cupboard to hang it. By the time she was done, Jackson had stripped down to his underwear, draping his shirt and trousers over the chair.

"Eddie told me to put this on." He held out a plastic packet.

Missy realized that it was a condom. She was happy that Eddie had thought about this detail that had not occurred to her.

"Let's get into bed first," she suggested. She quickly got naked, pulling her nightie over her shoulders and taking off her panties. After her months at the photo studio, she was not embarrassed about being in the nude before strange men.

Still in his underwear, Jackson helped her remove the bedcover from the bed and arrange the bedsheets. Quickly she snuggled underneath the bedsheets and waited for him.

The last time Missy had sex was with the Hollywood talent scout in Nashville. He was more experienced than her high school boyfriends. She hoped that Jackson would be equally mature in his lovemaking.

She watched him as he took off his vest and pair of boxers. He had the chiselled body of a boxer and his movements made him look like a lithe black panther. As he approached her, she noticed that his penis was erect and rock hard.

Once he joined her in bed, she made him lie on his back, taking the condom packet from him. Ripping the plastic cover, she took out the condom and expertly rolled it over his erection. Ever since high school, she insisted that her sex partner either bring condoms or be satisfied with a hand job.

"What is your favourite position?"

Jackson shrugged his shoulders. "I usually do it with me on the top."

Missy moved to lie on her back, spreading her legs. She remembered Eddie's request to take good care of Jackson and was determined to fake an orgasm, if needed.

When Jackson got on top of her, he hurt her when penetrating her. The pain soon gave way to pleasure as she became wet and his strokes went deeper. Jackson was now holding her tightly against him and kissing her on her neck and cheeks. She felt an orgasm building up and pressed against him for a clitoral release. A little later, she came again when she felt him throbbing inside her. It was all over in less than five minutes.

"You are absolutely amazing," he said while he lay on her. "This has been the best fuck of my life."

Now her nostrils picked up the odours of their sexual coupling – a mixture of his muskiness, her perfume and their sexual secretions. It was the first time that she had made love to a black man and experienced an orgasm such as intense when she touched herself.

"It was good for me too." She wondered if he knew that Eddie had paid her to sleep with him.

"I don't want this to end so quickly."

"What do you have in mind?"

"I want to go down on you."

"I'll need to wash up since we've just made love."

"Please, I've never kissed a white woman down there."

Missy got up and left for the bathroom. For a thousand dollars, he deserved what he wanted.

By the time she was back, he was waiting for her. She got back on the bed, closed her eyes and opened her thighs. Soon she felt his puckered lips lightly kissing her swollen sex, sending tiny convulsions racing back and forth along nerves already on fire. A wet tongue snaked out, unhurriedly lapping her moist slit. The tip curled over her hardened nub, repeatedly, making it burn. She felt her hips moving, driven by the waves building inside her. When she orgasmed, she clamped her thighs around Jackson's head.

"Wow that was something." Jackson looked up at her from between her legs. His lips were wet from her juices. "I like the way you taste."

Missy laughed as she caressed his head.

"You better wash up before you leave."

Jackson immediately got up and headed for the bathroom.

"It wasn't too bad. I actually enjoyed it," Missy thought to herself.

When Jackson returned, he was a different man. His earlier humble behaviour was replaced by an exuberant demeanour. He was now talking to her like any other male after sex.

"It was good for me. Was it good for you?"

"Sure, I enjoyed it too."

"You're the best."

"Thanks for the compliment. Do you have many girlfriends?"

"I've known some really nice coloured girls but sex with you was simply mind-blowing."

"Thank you. You're making a big deal of it."

"When will I see you again?"

"I don't know. You are in New York while I'm in LA."

"Perhaps you can come to New York. It will be a change from LA."

Missy had never thought of going to New York. Jackson talked about the things that he liked about New York and his dream of having a big fight in Madison Square Garden.

By now, although fully dressed, he seemed reluctant to leave.

"I'm tired. It must be the alcohol and love-making." Missy smiled, hoping that Jackson would take the hint.

"I'm sorry," Jackson immediately apologized. "You must promise that we will meet once again."

Missy found Jackson to be likeable but she wanted it to be a one-time thing. They had different interests. She wanted to be a movie star while he wanted to be a boxing champion. Perhaps their paths could cross if she went to New York. That would not very likely in the near future.

"Good-bye, Jackson. It was nice meeting you."

Jackson insisted on kissing her on the cheek before he left her.

As soon as she was alone, Missy thought about what had taken place. She had crossed the colour line by having sex with a black

24

man. For a Southern girl, it was unthinkable. Now she knew that she was capable of doing anything to make it in big time. Like Jackson, she also had a dream.

Chapter 5
Missy – Los Angeles 1965

"I've set up a meeting for you with Dave Gosner," Eddie announced when Missy joined him for Sunday brunch at the Café Del Rey.

"Who is Dave Gosner?"

"Dave is a fashion photographer from New York. He has come to LA to do some swimsuit shots for Sports Illustrated. I thought that it would be a good idea if you met him."

"Do you honestly think that I could qualify as a swimsuit model?"

"I have seen you in the buff and think that you are eminently qualified."

Eddie smiled in his usual charming way.

Missy had reluctantly accepted Eddie's invitation for a Sunday brunch since he had a habit of making unusual requests.

The last time when Eddie visited her at the photo studio, he invited her to a bar in Watts to meet a local council member, Herbert Parks. While they were having a drink, Missy noticed that Herb was constantly looking at her and it made her uncomfortable. After he left, Eddie explained that he owed Herb a few favours and requested her to have sex with him. This time he offered five hundred dollars and Missy gave in reluctantly only after Eddie's repeated requests.

"How did it go with Herb?" Eddie pulled out his billfold and gave her five one-hundred dollar bills.

"I don't think that I would like to meet him again." Missy recoiled at the memory of their date in a posh hotel near downtown Los Angeles.

"Why?" Eddie looked surprised. "Herb was happy to get some prime Southern white pussy."

"The second time around, he wanted to sodomize me," Missy said.

Eddie's face registered concern.

"Did you allow him?"

"I said no in a nice way and he did not pursue the matter."

Eddie looked relieved. Missy wondered whether it was because Herb had not complained.

"Herb Parks is one of those coloured politicians who want to get back at whitey by fucking their women in the ass," Eddie explained. Missy found his explanation to be gross.

"You shouldn't have set me up with him if you knew about his peccadilloes. I don't take it in the ass."

"I'll remember that for the next time," Eddie promised.

"Eddie, I am done with your dates. Why do you not set up your Afro-American friends with professional escorts? They would be more willing to oblige them with their special requests."

"Missy, you don't understand. These men have had their fill of those professional women with hard faces. They are looking something special – wholesome, girl-next-door types like you."

"If we get caught in one of those hotel raids that feature in newspapers, I could be booked for prostitution."

"You don't have to worry. We have protection."

"What kind of protection are you talking about?"

"I have connections with the local mob."

"How can they help?"

"Everybody works with the mob in this city. The politicians and the police take money from the bad boys. Nobody can do touch you as long as you are with me."

Missy was shocked. She had thought of Eddie as just an agent representing a few boxers. Now she realized that he was into bigger things.

"Do you have other wholesome girls in your stable?"

"Yes," Eddie admitted. "There are lots of out-of-state girls like you looking for a break in this city. I have three of them working for me because I provide sex for money or favours. It fits in with my other activities."

"I just have one more question for you, Eddie. Why have you never had sex with me?"

"I am from another generation, Missy. Besides, I am a married man. My wife would kill me if she knew that I was sleeping with one of my girls. I am not your usual kind of pimp." Eddie smiled.

"Hi, Eddie, it is good to see you again." A tall dark-haired man in a turtleneck pullover and blue trousers greeted them.

"Welcome to LA, Dave. It's been a while since we last met," Eddie said.

Eddie introduced Missy to Dave and they talked for a while. He had just flown in last night from New York.

"Let's go for the buffet," Eddie suggested. "We can talk business afterwards."

The three of them left for the buffet tables.

"You should try the oysters, the lobster risotto and the Burgundy snails," Eddie suggested as they surveyed the dishes on the table. Missy had never eaten oysters and snails. She decided to try them. Eddie was a man of the world.

The talk during the meal focused on the food. After surviving on burgers and pasta, it was a welcome change for Missy.

For dessert, Missy settled for a pineapple tart with rum raisin ice cream.

"I am proposing Missy as one of your models for your swimsuit assignment," Eddie said.

"I already have my list set up," Dave said. He looked at Missy. "Do you have any modelling experience?"

"She has been working as a glamour model for the past few months," Eddie hastily interposed.

"Do you have photos?"

"Yes. I even have a few nude shots so you can check out her body."

"Eddie, you are a rascal," David laughed. "Missy, you don't mind if I look at them?"

"Not at all," Missy replied.

"How about meeting up at the TIME-LIFE office tomorrow to look at your photo album?"

"We will be there," Eddie said. He winked at Missy.

Chapter 6
Missy – The Catskills 1967

"I've hardly woken up. Can't you wait for a while?" Missy protested as Jackson hovered over her, running his hand over her hips.

"I'm horny as hell."

Missy could not believe her ears. They had made love twice during the night and Jackson had pounded her for a long time before he came the second time. She was still sore and not sure whether she was ready for another round of lovemaking.

"We've just got this weekend and have to make up for lost time." Jackson was persistent with his hand now on her crotch.

"We have used up your stock of condoms." Missy realized that they had already had sex six times over the two days.

"I'll pull out before I come."

"Don't you think that we should wait until we have washed up?" Missy was playing for time.

"No. It will be more fun if we do it right away," Jackson persisted.

Since he was insistent, she decided to do it her way. She did not want his weight on top of her. In addition, she wanted to be in control to ensure that he did not come inside her.

"Let me get on top of you." Jackson seemed surprised at her request since they always made love in the missionary position up to now. He moved to lie on his back.

She climbed on top of him and ground down on his erection, taking it in slowly. Her pussy, already tender, felt stretched as she took in his bulbous head.

"This is a new one for me," he said, grinning. "For a change, you are doing all the work."

"There is a first time for everything," she gasped.

She drove herself down onto him faster and faster. Now she felt the familiar tingling between her legs and the welcome wetness to accommodate his size.

"It is hot in here," she said. The lodge in the Catskills had no air-conditioning. She could feel the sweat pricking her hairline.

She could feel the droplets dripping down from her armpits. She could feel the moisture spreading between her legs. She could smell herself; a rich and pungent odour.

"Look at us in the mirror. Don't we make a great couple?" Jackson pointed to the cupboard mirror.

The image of her white body riding a coal black man excited her. It looked like a scene from an interracial porn clip. She wondered what it must be like in being in one of those features. She got sore when Jackson fucked her just twice. How did porn actresses cope with doing it all the while? Maybe they just got used to it.

For a moment, she suddenly fantasized about another black man behind her, fucking her ass as she rode Jackson.

"I didn't know that it would be as wild as this," Jackson said, grasping her hips.

"Be careful," she said. "We're doing it bareback and I don't want you to come inside me."

"Play with yourself," Jackson begged. "I have never seen a woman do it."

She transferred her fingers to her clitoris, rubbing slowly in a circular motion. She was so wet that it was dripping out of her, soaking Jackson's pubic hair.

Feeling Jackson's penis starting to throb rhythmically inside her, she suddenly got off him.

"What's the matter?" Jackson was surprised.

She moved towards his pelvis and started to stroke him.

"I will jack you off."

"Please take me in your mouth," he begged. She was surprised at his bold request.

She got her mouth around him and tasted her own juices. She could feel him throbbing and knew that it would not be long for him now.

She became reckless. She used her mouth in a way she had never done before, tonguing and sucking him while she cupped his scrotum. It just took him a couple of minutes to come, his hot seed filling her mouth and dripping over her chin and neck.

"I'm sorry," he said. "But you were great." He was looking at her with affection.

Perhaps this was the first time that a woman had fellated him to completion. She sensed a change in his attitude towards her. Earlier he seemed respectful. Now he was demanding in his sexual preferences.

She was surprised at her own wantonness to satisfy him. The public taboo in sexual relations between white women and black men made her clandestine trysts with Jackson even more exciting. It seemed as if being with a black man made her less inhibited to catering to her partner's sexual fantasies. Sex with Jackson was about pure lust.

Sitting up, she picked up the counterpane to wipe her mouth. Her nostrils picked up the whiff in the still air, a combination of Jackson's muskiness and her sexual odour. The bedsheet, sodden with their sweat and her secretions, was mute testimony to their lovemaking.

She admired her naked blonde body in the cupboard mirror. Behind her, she saw Jackson's black body with his thick penis lying flat over his stomach.

"Beauty and the beast," she thought. She dismissed the thought. Jackson, his body glistening in the sunshine, looked more like a black Adonis.

"I need a shower." She got up to leave for the bathroom.

"I will join you." Jackson followed her.

A shower together would be another first for them.

* * * * *

"We've just got one more day before my training camp starts."

Missy and Jackson were walking along a mountain trail a little away from the lodge.

"How long will you be training?" Missy knew that she would not be able to see Jackson during the period prior to his fight.

"I wonder how he will manage with the no sex rule," she thought.

"It will be six weeks. I'm expecting the entire crew to be here tomorrow."

"How many people will be there?" She imagined that the lodge would be teeming with males tomorrow.

31

"There will be around ten people, counting my sparring partners, trainer, masseur, medical specialist and a cook."

"Wow, I didn't realise that the team would be so big. Who is picking up the tab?"

"Eddie and some promoters are putting up the money." Jackson did not want to say any more.

"They'll probably get a share of your prize money." Missy wanted to know more.

"It'll be around forty percent. There will be enough left for me."

Missy pondered how much Jackson would get after deductions for expenses. The weekly rental for the ten-room hunting lodge must alone be over a thousand dollars.

"I'm planning to take a break after the fight. Why don't we take a trip to the Bahamas?"

"I can't take any time off, Jackson. You know that Dave has this contract with Matchless Cosmetics and will be shooting a few commercials this fall."

"I'm sure that you can arrange to take a few days off. We will need to celebrate."

Missy had mixed emotions of admiration and concern. Jackson, the eternal optimist, was already behaving as if he had won the fight against the defending champion. He was also talking as if they were already a steady couple.

"No, it is out of question." Missy decided to be firm and end any further talk on this topic.

"Eddie thinks that we'll make a great couple."

"I think that this has to be between you and me. Eddie's opinion does not count."

Missy resented that Jackson had mentioned Eddie's name. Eddie, as her agent, was already taking a fifteen percent commission on her earnings as Dave's model. Ever since Matchless Cosmetics had selected her as Miss Matchless for their mascara collection, she had been making good money. Their two-year contract was soon ending and she needed to hire a lawyer to negotiate better terms.

"Eddie has a high opinion of you. If it hadn't been for Eddie, we would not have met."

Missy wondered how Jackson could be so naïve. Did he really think that she fell for him after their first meeting in Las Vegas?

"I can't do this anymore," Missy thought to herself.

"We have known each other for more than two years and I like you. Eddie, we're just friends, nothing more."

"I love you, Missy. You have to give our relationship a little more time. It will build up."

"We live in two different worlds. You are a boxer and I am a model. Each of us is working towards a professional goal."

"I am sure that you will give up modelling once we are together. You won't need to work."

Missy could not believe her ears. Was Jackson proposing marriage? Surely, he did not believe that they were already a couple just because they had sex a few times.

"Look, Jackson, I love my work. Dave has given me a few good breaks since he selected me for the Sports Illustrated swimsuit issue. There is no question of me giving up my modelling career in New York."

Jackson was silent for a few minutes. Missy sensed that he was trying to absorb the consequences of what she was saying. For the rest of the trail, they did not speak until they reached the lodge.

* * * * *

When they reached the porch, they saw a bulky man with two suitcases.

"Hi Chris. Have you been waiting long?" Jackson shook hands with the man.

"Missy, this is Chris. He is my trainer and sparring partner."

Chris looked a bit embarrassed, as if he had not expected to see Jackson with a white woman.

"Missy will be driving back to New York this afternoon."

Chris looked relieved. His heavy-lidded eyes and face crinkled into a friendly smile as they shook hands.

"Chris, did you bring the camera?"

"Yes, it's in my hand bag." He walked to his luggage, picked up his handbag and took out a camera.

"Thanks, Chris." He took the camera and ran his fingers over its polished surface.

"What kind of camera do you have?" Missy was curious.

"This is a Polaroid camera. It takes instant pictures."

"It looks like a new model. I have seen older models years ago at the photo studio in LA."

"We will be using the camera to take photos of my sparring partners during the training camp," Jackson explained. "Chris will also be posting photos of the mountain trail for our daily run."

They talked for a while about the training schedule for the coming week.

"Chris, can you take a photo of Missy and me?" Surprised by Jackson's sudden request, Missy demurred.

"I am not looking my best and we are both sweaty again after our walk."

Chris took the camera and looked at Missy for askance.

"Come on, Missy. Be a sport." Jackson gave a desperate look.

"Alright, you take just one photo." She was feeling guilt about her ambivalent feelings towards Jackson and wanted to make it up to him. Meanwhile Chris was fiddling with the camera.

Jackson put his arm around her shoulder and pulled her towards him.

"OK, Chris. Take a shot."

Chris took a picture and they waited for the image to roll out from the camera.

"It's too far away. How about taking a close-up?" Jackson put the photo in his pocket.

This time Jackson moved his face close to her face and it was too late for her to pull away.

Each time Jackson looked at the result and then urged Chris to take a new one. They stopped only when Missy protested. It was when Jackson had suddenly grabbed her and Chris had taken a photo of Jackson kissing her. By this time, Jackson had a dozen photos of them in various embraces in his pocket.

Missy was uncomfortable. Those photos were dynamite. Chris would probably babble about them to the other people in Jackson's training camp. They would know about Jackson's white girlfriend, a New York fashion model. She hoped that Jackson would keep the collection for himself only. If those photos became public, her career as a Matchless Cosmetics ambassadress would be finished. She would get them back one day.

Chapter 7
Missy – Los Angeles 1975

"I have hearing some ugly rumours."

Martin Grover, the boss of MGA Studio, had summoned Missy and her agent, Jake Bronstein, to his office urgently.

"What kind of rumours?" Jake sounded anxious.

"Rona Barrett called me the other day. She is planning to do an item on you." Martin gave Missy a stern look.

Missy's heart beat faster. Her mouth went dry. Rona was one of LA's top gossip columnists. She also had a cosy relationship with Martin.

"Rona tells me that a little bird saw a white Hollywood actress in the company of a black boxer at a Sunday brunch in LA."

"What's that got to do with us?" Jake shrugged his shoulders.

Martin ignored him.

"Do you happen to be in a relationship with a black fighter?" He looked at Missy.

"Well, I happen to know one on a social basis. We met through a common friend." Missy hoped that the answer would satisfy Martin.

"Would that fighter happen to be the current welterweight champion?"

"Yes," Missy admitted. "Jackson Coots is just an old friend."

"Can you imagine what will happen should Rona print her little bird story in her gossip column? It will be just a matter of time before people find out about you and your boxer friend."

"It was nothing, just a meal together. Eddie Conklin, a common friend, had me over for brunch at the Marina Del Rey café." Missy tried to brush it off as an unimportant event.

Martin pushed a button on his telephone set. A tall, blonde woman, dressed in a black costume and high heels, walked in. She carried a notepad.

"Ask Joe to get me some dope on Eddie Conklin."

The woman wrote the name on a notepad, spelling out 'Conklin'.

"Is this urgent?"

"Tell him that I am in a meeting with Missy McGuire and Jake Bronstein."

"Should he give you a call?"

"Yes. Put him through straightaway."

"Is that all, Mr Grover?"

Martin nodded and the woman left the room.

"Did you know about this relationship?" Martin gave Jake a sharp look.

"No." Jake looked questioningly at Missy.

"Jake didn't know anything about Jackson and me." Missy felt that it was her duty to defend her agent.

"Look, Jake. We will be shortly releasing Missy's new film. This is not a good time for Rona to publish an innuendo about a blonde star and a black boxer."

"What do you want us to do?"

"I want you to stop seeing Jackson," Martin said, looking at Missy.

"This is my private life. You can't tell me what to do," Missy protested.

"Look, Missy, you don't understand. The studio has put in a lot of money in building you up as a star and wants to protect its investment."

"What has that got to do with Jackson?"

"How would it look if fans found out that their favourite blonde sex bomb is having an affair with a black man? They will ban your film in the South. Don't you see the consequences?"

"I agree with Martin," Jake concurred. "We need to keep this thing under wraps."

"I can get Rona to kill this item. She owes me a favour," Martin said.

"That's good," Jake said, looking relieved.

"Missy, you have to be careful in future. Please do not do anything to hurt your image before the launch. By the way, did you see the final cut?"

"Yes," Missy was happy to change the subject. "I think that my songs came out very well."

"I agree," Martin said. "If you must know, we used a playback singer to replace your voice."

36

"Why?" Missy was upset that the studio had done this without checking with her.

"Pierre Stern felt that your voice quivered during the high notes. Margie Nixon sang for you." Missy felt that Pierre, the music director, should have told her about his reservations.

"I can't believe it. She sounded like me."

"Margie is a professional. She is good at blending in other people's voices."

"What if a gossip columnist like Rona finds out that the studio used a playback singer for my songs?"

"Nobody will ever know," Martin said smugly.

"Are you sure?"

"Margie's contract has a non-disclosure clause. She will never get another contract in Hollywood if she tells anybody that she was your playback singer in the film."

"Isn't that hard on her?"

"I agree but she knows that our money is riding on you. We have spent more than ten million dollars on this film and will be premiering it in London and New York."

"I think that this was my best role and the film should do well."

"I agree," Martin nodded. "The combination of a blonde sex symbol and an English Academy Award winner is unbeatable."

Missy winced when Martin described her as a 'sex symbol'. Her first film with the studio had been in an upscale skin flick but she had progressed over the past five years. The studio had even hired an exclusive acting coach for her.

The three talked for a while about the film launch while Jake noted Martin's instructions for Missy's tour to promote the film. Martin was in an exuberant mood and had even lit up a cigar.

When the phone rang, Martin continued talking for a while before he picked up the receiver.

"Put him through," he said.

"Hello, Joe. Thanks for getting back to me so soon." Martin listened for a while to the voice on the phone. His face turned serious.

"You are saying that this guy, Eddie Conklin, is Jackson Coot's agent and has connections with the mob. What else do you have on him?"

They talked for a while with Martin asking further questions about Eddie Conklin. After he hung up, Martin turned to Missy.

"The news is not good. Your friend, Eddie Conklin, is a petty gangster. He is a front man for the mob in managing the numbers racket in Afro-American neighbourhoods. They say that his connections with the mob helped him set up fights for Jackson Coots."

"I did not know that he was so involved with the mob," Missy said.

"I don't want you to have any more to do with either Eddie Conklin or Jackson Coots." Martin made it sound like an order.

"It might sound strange if I suddenly stop receiving their calls."

"I will make it easy for you. They won't bother you anymore," Martin said in a determined voice.

"How do you mean?"

"Joe has his contacts with some of the boys in the mob." Martin's voice dropped to a whisper. "They will warn Eddie to stay away from you."

"One more thing," Martin continued. "The same applies for Jackson. They will break every bone in his body if he ever tries to see you again."

Missy saw Martin in a new light. The wooden wall behind him had an array of photographs of him posing with film stars and politicians. There was a photo with Martin with President Nixon in the White House. Now she realized that Martin was just as powerful as the President was.

"I have a few suggestions until this thing blows over," Martin said, looking at Jake. "I want Missy to leave LA and fly to London for the premiere. It will be a royal performance. Afterwards she should enjoy a holiday on the French Riviera. She deserves it."

Missy felt that Martin was treating her as any other paid employee. In a way, he was justified. She was under contract to the studio and they had invested in building her up as a star. Now Martin was protecting his investment, which could depreciate should her star rating drop at the box office.

"How soon can you fly to London?" Jake asked Missy. Always considerate, he wanted to involve her in the discussion.

"I will need a few days," Missy replied.

"I want her out of LA while Jackson is still in town," Martin broke in.

"Let's fly to Las Vegas today," Jake suggested.

Missy was reluctant. She had wanted to phone either Eddie or Jackson to tell them about her meeting with Martin. This way they would understand that why she could not see them anymore.

"That's a good idea." Martin called for his secretary and told her to make flight bookings and hotel reservations for Missy and Jake. He then got up to signal that the meeting was over.

Once they were outside Martin's office, Jake turned to Missy.

"I don't want to know anything about Jackson Coots. Just promise me that you will never contact him ever again."

Missy nodded. In her heart, she knew that she preferred the role of a Hollywood star than being the white wife of a black boxing champion. Martin had done something that she had not really dared to do. He had terminated her relationship with Jackson.

Chapter 8
Jason – Las Vegas 2005

"We have two rooms reserved in the name of Mr Jason Grant." The receptionist looked at her computer screen. Jason noticed that she was a tall redhead with blue eyeshadow.

"We could share a room." Bubba whispered, nudging Jason on his rib cage.

"Relax, man. We are celebrating," Jason replied. He had his own reason for booking two separate rooms at the Stardust Resort and Casino.

The receptionist placed a registration form on the front desk.

"You will need to fill this out and sign at the bottom." She gave Jason a charming smile.

"May I have your credit card?"

Jason pulled out his billfold and handed over his brand new Visa card.

"When did you get this credit card?" Bubba asked in a barely audible murmur.

"Yesterday," Jason replied. "I went to the bank and collected it before we left for the airport."

"Thank you, Mr Grant." The receptionist returned his credit card. Jason looked admiringly at her. She had twinkling light brown eyes.

"I have given you rooms on the same floor," she said, handing each of them their room cards.

The two men took the elevator to their rooms on the tenth floor.

"This is going to cost you a packet," Bubba said.

"Remember, we are celebrating my new job," Jason said.

"Yes but you didn't have to book two rooms."

"Don't worry. This shindig is on me." Jason just wanted a wild weekend before starting on his new job with the Lisa Donovan Talent Agency.

"Let's meet at the pool in half-an-hour," Jason suggested, as they stood before their rooms. "We've got an hour of sunshine left."

Once in his room, Jason opened his suitcase and picked out his swimming costume. He could not wait to get to the pool.

* * * * *

Jason and Bubba were sitting on sun chairs around the hotel's 'Big Dipper' pool, eyeing the women sitting around the pool and in the water.

"I don't see any sistas," Bubba said. "There are only honky females around here."

"What have you got against good looking white girls?"

"I'd feel more comfortable if we could hook up with a couple of brown gals. We are the only black guys around here."

"Come on. We are here to have a good time."

Jason got up. Seeing people standing in the water along the periphery of the large, odd-shaped pool, he selected a place next to three girls. He sat with his feet in the water.

"Hi, I am Jason from LA. Is this your first time in Las Vegas?"

One of the girls looked at him. She replied, "Yes."

"Where are you from?"

"Omaha, Nebraska." The other two girls on her side stared at Jason.

"How long will you be in Las Vegas?"

"We are here for a week." The girl turned away and the three started talking among themselves. Obviously, they were not interested in starting a conversation with him. He looked around to see if Bubba was watching and relieved to see that he was reading a newspaper.

"OK. Have a nice time." The girls did not even bother to reply.

Jason walked back to his sun chair and Bubba put down his newspaper.

"How was it?"

"It was nothing special. I just talked to some girls from a hick town in the Midwest."

"You are a fast worker."

"What about you?"

"Man, Jaquelin is jealous as hell. She'd kill me if she ever heard we had chatted up with a couple of pink toes in Vegas."

"Don't tell me that you're going steady with Jaquelin?"

"I went to her house last night and she gave me some of that candy, if you know what I mean." Bubba smirked. Jason remembered that Jaquelin was just as dark as Bubba but friendly and good-natured. They made a good couple.

"I like what I'm seeing here," Jason said, as he scanned the people lying on sun chairs around the pool.

"Don't tell me that you are lusting for some white meat." Bubba was taunting him.

"I sure am." Jason looked Bubba in the eye. "Those niggas that say that they find honky babes unattractive are either kidding themselves or gays."

"Are you saying that we blacks are all lusting after white flesh? That simply is not true."

"Have you ever made it out with a white chick?"

"No and I want to keep it that way. The only white girls that go with brothers were skaggy ones. They are plump hoochies."

"Not all white women are hos. Look at that bird over there on the sun chair next to the shower. She has got class." The blonde woman with a heavy bust got up to take a shower.

"She has a body like a Coke bottle," Jason added admiringly.

"You can't think of anything but white poontang," Bubba jeered.

"I'm going to get myself one of those vanillas."

"Are you serious?" Bubba looked at Jason with disbelief.

"I mean it."

"Good luck."

"What about you?"

"Count me out. I am ugly as ten mofos."

Jason was surprised that Bubba had such a low sense of self-esteem when it came to his physical looks. Perhaps it had to do with his dark skin and overweight.

"I would suggest that we split after dinner. You can play the slots while I will look for a white hoochie mama."

"Just be careful. Some of those dolls are fake rip-offs who will make a play for your wallet."

"I'll manage," Jason said, looking at his watch. "Let's sit here for another twenty minutes before we shower and have a bite."

* * * * *

42

After dinner, Jason left Bubba in the casino and returned to his room.

He took out his laptop and connected it to the room telephone. Once he logged in on the hotel's network, he surfed on the Internet, searching for female escort web sites.

There was a wide choice of web sites but most of the escorts featured looked like street whores with heavily made-up faces, short skirts and boots. Finally, he chanced upon a web site featuring mature women. He fancied an older white woman who had an elegant look and went under the name of Liz. She reminded him of Stacey, his first grade school teacher. It had always been his fantasy to make love to a woman like her. He called the number listed and a calm voice at the other end answered at the other end.

"This is Liz. How can I help you?"

"This is Mr Grant and I am at the Stardust Resort and Casino."

"It is ten minutes away from where I am."

"I would like a house call."

"It will be a hundred dollars, payable in advance in cash."

"What kind of services will you be offering?"

"It will be full service with oral stimulation and sex with protection. The time limit is one hour." The woman's voice sounded cultured.

"How soon can you come?"

"I am free and can be over there in half-an-hour."

"My room number is five hundred twenty."

"I have got it." The voice repeated the room number and the hotel name.

"That's right."

"Thank you." The woman hung up.

Twenty minutes later, there was a soft knock on his door. Jason opened the door and saw an elegant fiftyish white woman in a smart black dress and dignified three-inch black high heel shoes.

"I am sorry. I think that I have knocked on the wrong door."

"No. I am expecting you," Jason said with an air of confidence.

The woman looked at him in disbelief. Suddenly Jason had his doubts. With her lacquered hair, string of pearls and expensive

Cartier watch, she could be a guest returning to her hotel room, expecting her husband to open the door.

"May I know your name?"

"I am Jason Grant."

"Do you have an ID?"

Jason was irritated but he pulled out his wallet and showed his driver's licence to the woman.

"Oh, I am at the right place."

"Perhaps you were surprised to see a black man?" Jason hoped she would be honest.

"No, it is not like that," the woman demurred. "You sounded much older on the phone but you are young. Normally it is the older men who call me for my services."

"Why don't you come in?" Jason opened the door wider. The woman hesitated and then stepped inside the room.

Jason led her to one corner of the room where there were two chairs and a table.

"I hope that you do not mind that I am young and black?"

"At my age, I prefer older men since they are more considerate and gentlemanly."

Jason interpreted her definition of considerate to be a synonym for generous.

"What about black men?"

"In my business, we have to be careful about black men. There could be pimps looking for women to work for them."

"Do I look like a pimp?"

"I think not." The woman smiled.

"We also try and avoid young black men from the ghettoes. They think that it is their right to be rough with a woman to get their money's worth. There are all types of tourists in this town."

Jason hoped that she would not guess that he came from Watts in LA.

"I promise not to be rough. By the way, my name is Jason."

"I'm Liz." The woman leaned forward. "I am sorry but I must ask you for the money. It will be a hundred dollars."

Jason took out his wallet again and gave her a hundred dollar bill.

She stuffed the hundred-dollar bill in her handbag and stood up.

"Thank you." Without a word, she started undressing, laying her clothes neatly over a chair.

Jason' heart pumped violently against his rib cage, as he watched Liz undress. She shucked off her shoes, unzipped her dress, took off her brassiere and pulled down her panty hose. Now she was naked, a middle-aged woman looking vulnerable with her wrinkles and bumps. Jason noticed her sagging breasts, rounded stomach and thick thighs. What excited him was the expanse of creamy white skin, unblemished by sun-tanned lines. He had an instant erection.

Dressing in a hurry, he dumped his clothes on the second chair.

"My, you are a big boy," the woman said.

The woman sat on the bed and beckoned him to sit next to her. She already had a condom in her hand, which she expertly slid a condom over his erect penis.

She lay on her back, allowing him the sight of her white thighs spread open with her delicate pink lips peeking from her slit. Jason could not wait for a minute more. He mounted her and she guided him inside her. It was a delicious feeling to be engulfed in her softness. Inhaling her floral perfume, he kissed her on her cheeks while holding her tightly against him. He increased his strokes and she responded by putting her legs around his back to allow him to penetrate her deeper.

"I am coming," he gasped, experiencing a powerful orgasm. His ejaculations went on for longer than usual. Totally spent, Jason collapsed on her soft body.

Liz was gentle and patient even after it was over. She let him lie on her for a few minutes, stroking his back. When he got off her, she expertly pulled of his condom and left for the bathroom. Returning with a moist hand towel, she gently swabbed his flaccid penis and then dried him.

"Thanks, that was great. We still have forty minutes and I am ready for seconds." Jason looked at her expectantly. He was now ready for a blowjob, which he expected was part of the one-hour full service.

"I'm afraid but you are entitled to only one shot," Liz said sweetly..

"I thought that I had paid for an hour."

"It is either one hour or one ejaculation, whatever comes first."

She walked to the corner of the room and started dressing.

Jason was tempted to offer another hundred dollars but he was running short of cash.

"Perhaps we can meet another time?"

"You have my phone number. I am available from 2 p.m. till 2 a.m."

She was now fully dressed and getting into her shoes.

"Stay in bed. I will let myself out."

She walked to the door and undid the safety latch. Waving to Jason, she let herself out and quietly closed the door behind her.

Jason was happy and frustrated. His first encounter with a white woman had lived up to his expectations. He was only disappointed that it was over so soon.

"I missed out on my blowjob," he thought. If only he had insisted on her to go down on him before she put on the condom. He pictured her pink lips sucking on his black cock. The visual image was enough to give him an urge to masturbate.

He had come to Las Vegas to have sex with a white woman and Liz had initiated him into the joys of interracial sex. Now he was looking forward to his new job and access to a seemingly unlimited supply of willing white females.

Chapter 10
Jason – Los Angeles 2006

"We need to have a chat about a couple of issues."

Jason was in John Gardner's office and had a foreboding that it was going to be a tough talk.

"I have a couple of expense vouchers for cabs. Don't you have a car?"

"Those expense notes are for the trips I made to Harry Stern's office before I purchased a car."

"In future, please use your car for in-city travel and we will reimburse you on the basis of your mileage. You will need my prior approval if you want to use a cab."

"OK, I will approve your expenses." He picked up his phone and pushed three buttons.

"Hello, Linda. Can you please come to my office?"

A minute later Linda Murphy, the office manager, entered the office. Jason smiled nervously in her direction but she greeted him with a curt good morning.

"Thanks for drawing my attention to Jason's expense vouchers," John spoke to Linda.

"White bitch", Jason swore under his breath. She had sent his expense notes to John.

"What is your decision?" Linda bent forward over the table, her sundress exposing the top of her creamy breasts. Jason's heart beat faster even while loathing the woman.

"This time we will okay his cab expenses but I have told him to use his own car in future."

Jason felt that Linda looked disappointed. He wondered if she had something against him.

While Linda was talking with John, he looked at her. He preferred women like Linda with their silky hair, fair skin and light eyes. Perhaps classy blonde-haired women were off-limits for ghetto boys like him. As the token black in this lily-white organisation, he had better be careful.

After Linda finished talking with John, she turned away, revealing long, shapely legs in high heels. He experienced a hard on, cursing himself for lusting after a white woman who treated him in this derogatory manner.

"We have another issue on our agenda," John said. "This concerns the Harry Stern contract."

"I have been working on it and we are almost finished."

"You have been working on it almost since six months and we still have not signed him up."

"My problem is that Harry's lawyer is always coming up with new objections and our lawyers are now working on the latest version."

"If we don't move fast, Harry may sign up with another agent."

"I am doing my best."

"May be your best isn't good enough." John's rebuke hurt Joshua. He had been putting in extra hours on the job.

"What do you want me to do?"

"I want to put another person on this project to help you."

"I can manage on my own since the contract is almost done," Jason protested.

"We need to close the deal by next week. Annabelle will work with you."

Normally Jason would have been happy to work with Annabelle who joined the company at the same time as him. On this occasion, it seemed almost like she would take over the project.

"I don't think that it is necessary." Jason described the work that he had already done while John listened, drumming his fingers on the table.

"The decision has been taken. Please meet Annabelle on Monday and brief her on the contract. She will work with the lawyers."

Jason felt the air sucking out of the room. He could hardly breathe. John had decided to give the project to Annabelle and there was no appeal.

"OK, I will meet her," he said in a resigned manner.

"One thing more," John said. "Your probation period is coming to an end in a fortnight's time. Let's hope that everything is settled in time for a favourable review."

There was an implied threat in his words. He wanted the Harry Stern contract signed at the earliest.

"That will be all for now. You can go and collect your cash from Harriet."

John turned his attention back to his computer screen.

"Right, John, you can count on me." He got up.

"I hope that it will work out." John looked at him briefly before returning his attention to his screen.

Jason wondered if John was a white racist, who could not tolerate the idea of a black man tarnishing one of 'their' women. Perhaps he had exacerbated the situation by flirting with the women in the office and acting as the stereotype of the black alpha male who got by in life because he was sporting fit and a supposed super-stud.

After leaving John's office, Jason headed for Harriet's workplace. The company cashier sat behind a grilled enclosure.

"I understand that Linda has given you my expense vouchers. John has signed them."

Jason let his gaze linger on Harriet's dark hair tinged with grey strands, plucked eyebrows and hazel eyes.

"Yes, I just got them. There are three notes. "

Harriet scanned the expense notes, her eyes narrowing behind her spectacles.

"Yes. John has signed them. Let me do a quick total." Harriet mumbled the amounts as she computed the total in her head.

"The total is one hundred and forty dollars. Can I give you a hundred and two twenties?"

"That will be nice."

Jason melted when Harriet gave him a warm smile, as she handed him the money.

Harriet reminded him of Stacey, his first grade school teacher. He had fallen in love with her, deciding to marry a white woman like her when he grew up. This innocent puppy love gave way to adolescent sexual fantasies when he got glimpses of Stacey's panties and her white thighs. He wondered whether Harriet also wore laced panties like Stacey. Damn, he was getting a hard on again.

Jason decided to go to the mailroom to see if the revised draft Harry Stern contract had arrived. Gina was the one white girl who was always nice to him.

Jason found Gina to be pretty but overweight. She had the beginning of a double chin and heavy breasts. He had never seen her legs because she wore a kaftan to hide her stout figure.

"How is our basketball hero doing today?"

Gina was aware that he had played as point guard with the LBSU basketball team. The other white women showed little interest when he talked about his glorious past in college basketball games.

"I haven't touched a ball since I've been working in this sweatshop."

Gina laughed.

"You should take time off to see the team practise. The old gang would be glad to see you."

Jason just shrugged his shoulders.

"Do you have any mail from Harry Stern for me?"

While Gina scanned the letters on her table, Jason wondered whether she had been a basketball groupie.

"Nope, there is nothing from Harry's office."

"Thanks, Gina."

"Are you going to the LBSU game this weekend?"

Jason felt that she might be angling for a date. He decided to play it safe.

"No, I have a couple of other things lined up."

He was not too keen to be with Gina in front of his former teammates. Most of them joked that only fat white girls went out with black men.

"What a pity. This game is going to be a clincher."

Gina gave Jason a pleading look. Jason just shrugged his shoulders.

He thought about Jamal, a teammate who had a live-in chubby white girlfriend. The relationship lasted just six months. As soon as he became a professional player, Jamal dumped his partner for a Hollywood starlet.

"We'll make it some other time." He winked at Gina.

Jason thought Gina was nice but had no class. The Swedish blonde model who had been married to Tiger Woods had class.

Black celebrities usually had trophy white wives as markers of their success. If Tiger could pull it off then he should also aspire for the same.

On the way back to his desk, Jason spotted Annabelle kneeling at the copying machine, loading a stack of white paper. Her jeans had ridden below to expose the string of her black thong indented against her white back.

He felt a slight erection building up in his trousers.

"How is it going with your assignment?"

Annabelle stood up and turned to face Jason.

"I've got it up to here," she replied, raising her hand up to her forehead. "John has asked for more changes in the Gloria West contract."

Jason moved closer to Annabelle, admiring her chestnut brown mop of hair, blushing pink cheeks and barely visible lipstick.

"I'm almost finished on the Harry Stern contract. John told me that you would be helping me out." Jason observed her carefully to see her reaction.

"Yes, John told me that you needed a back-up." She looked a bit embarrassed. Jason realized that she knew that she would be taking over the assignment.

Annabelle smiled nervously, her mouth opening to reveal a set of perfectly capped white teeth. Jason appreciated Annabelle's casual chic appearance combining designer jeans with high heels. She was also an intern but could seemingly afford to splurge on clothes.

"John told me to meet you to discuss the Harry Stern contract."

"I need to have a preliminary meeting with John before we meet. Let's discuss on Tuesday." Annabelle quickly turned away, looking in the direction of John's glass cubicle office. Jason saw John staring at them. She was not in a mood to continue the conversation.

"Bye for now," Jason quickly said, raising his hand and moving away.

Back at his desk, Jason was feeling depressed. Except for Gina, most of the office staff seemed courteous but reserved with him. He had worked hard for six months on the Harry Stern

51

contract and the agency had still not been able to sign up the television series star. His future looked dim.

The telephone rang but he waited for six rings before picking up the receiver.

"Hello! Lisa Donovan Talent Agency! Jason Grant speaking! May I help you?"

Recognising the voice at the other end, he adopted an apologetic tone. "Hello Mrs Donovan. I am sorry for having kept you waiting."

"Good morning Jason. Can you come over to my office now?" The voice was polite and soft.

"I am coming there."

Taking his yellow legal pad, Jason made for Lisa's office. The company CEO usually talked to John, his immediate boss. With his six-month probation period ending, did they want to fire him?

Jason tensed, as he stood outside Lisa's office. He had once met Lisa when he was in John's office and found her to be very attractive. On this occasion, he had to put his erotic fantasies aside and be on his best behaviour because this woman held the key to his future.

Jason knocked, opened the door and walked towards Lisa Donovan who was sitting at the far end behind a big glass-topped desk. The office, with its wood panelling, abstract paintings and a view of Los Angeles from the windows, impressed him. This was real big time.

Jason noticed that Lisa looking at him with a bemused expression. "Sit down, young man!"

Chapter 11
Lisa - Los Angeles 2006

Lisa looked at Jason with interest as he sank into the big leather chair opposite her.

This was the second time she was meeting this black intern.

"My God, this is a beautiful hunk of a man," she thought to herself

With his smooth black skin, Jason reminded her of Wesley Snipes. Only his close-cropped curling hair and full, lush mouth gave him a sensual look. He also had the most startling eyes, a light brown that contrasted with his dusky skin.

Right now he was looking at her, those clear brown eyes intense, questioning. She shivered.

"Well, Jason, this is the second time that we are meeting and I want to know if you are enjoying your work at our agency?"

"I'm helping John with his clients and the work has been challenging."

Lisa found his answer to be guarded. John had told her that Jason had potential. The only problem was that he enjoyed spending time with his female co-workers, playing the role of the alpha black male.

"How are you getting along with your colleagues?"

"John has assigned Annabelle to help me with the Harry Stern contract."

Lisa recalled the attractive young brunette who had been hired at the same time as Jason.

She had hired Jason on the recommendation of a family friend, the dean of LBSU College. The other board members also thought that it was good to have a black intern if the agency decided to do public relations work for clients from minority communities.

"I think that John has a good team with Annabelle and you,"

"Thank you, Mrs Donovan."

Jason looked at her questioningly. He was probably trying to guess the reason why he had been called for this interview.

Lisa decided not to waste any time and get to the point immediately.

"I have a new assignment for you," she announced. "Can you transfer Harry Stern's contract project to Annabelle?"

"Can't this wait until next week? Harry is sending us the final draft and we'll be signing the contract shortly."

Lisa was secretly pleased with Jason's protest. It showed that he was attached to his work.

"No, please hand over everything to Annabelle by this afternoon."

Lisa said those words with a tone of finality and then noticed Jason slump into his chair and look with exasperation at the ceiling.

"Come on, Jason, I have a reason for my decision."

"Did John complain about me?"

"No. This decision has nothing to do with John."

"You've to understand that Harry Stern and his agent have been asking for change after change. I'm almost there. Please let me finish the assignment."

Lisa melted when she saw Jason's pleading brown eyes. She imagined comforting him by holding his head against her bosom. The thought sent a hot flush through her body.

"Is anything wrong? Please let me know if John has complained about me," Jason asked.

Lisa saw him looking anxiously at her.

"No, John is just a little impatient," Lisa replied reassuringly. "He realizes that Harry is a tough prospect and his lawyers are holding out for a good deal."

She saw Jason sigh with relief. Still he looked concerned.

"What about Harry?" Jason asked. "He might want to know why Annabelle has taken over from me."

Lisa gave him a reassuring smile.

"Annabelle and John will handle Harry. You say that the job is almost finished."

"Okay," said Jason. "So it's all been settled. What do you have in mind for me?"

"Our agency will now be branching into a new line of business and I have decided that you are the right person for this assignment."

Lisa got up from her chair, walked around her table and gestured to Jason to move to the round table in the alcove of her office.

As Lisa sat on the low sofa, her skirt slid over her knees.

She noticed Jason lower his head. Was he trying to take a quick peek?

"Jason, is everything alright?"

"Yes," he replied hurriedly, embarrassed at being caught in the act. He looked briefly at her and then cast his eyes downwards at her black patent leather high heel shoes.

Lisa smoothened out her skirt demurely. She leaned forward and gave him an expectant look.

"Can I trust you to be discrete?" she asked.

Jason nodded but looked confused. Lisa realized that he was wondering whether she was referring to his attempt to look up her skirt.

"This concerns a confidential project."

"Nobody else is supposed to know?"

"Well, John knows about it but I would rather that we handle this at our level."

"Does this mean that I should deal directly with you only?"

"Yes."

"OK, you can count on my discretion."

"Melissa McGuire is coming into town day after tomorrow," Lisa said.

Lisa paused for a moment and noticed Jason looking awestruck. She was pleased that Jason had recognized the film star's name.

"We had signed her as our client six months ago and she has just finished shooting a film in Toronto. Now she will be in Los Angeles for two days for a publicity photo shoot prior to the release of the film."

Jason gasped.

"The tabloids call her Missy and she retired several years ago from the movie industry. Is she making a comeback?"

"Well, it is a kind of comeback."

"Wow, that's great. What's my assignment?"

Lisa paused for a minute. She looked down at her shoes and then said, "It is a little sensitive and I'll need you to be absolutely discrete."

"You can count on me, Mrs Donovan."

"Your job will be to accompany Missy during her stay in town and make sure that she turns up for the photo shoot."

"That's no big deal. I'm honoured that you have selected me for this job."

Jason looked excited. Lisa imagined that he was already salivating at the prospect of being with an attractive blonde although she was old enough to be his grandmother.

"This assignment makes up for the disappointment in not being able to close the Harry Stern deal."

Lisa crossed her legs and her skirt rode up again. This time Jason did not look downward. She saw that he was being discrete in other ways too.

"Well, there's a problem and I don't know how to put it across to you. Lisa has featured in an interracial romance film and she has been nervous about it from the start."

"Interracial, like she has worked with a black co-star?"

Jason looked at her expectantly. Lisa could see that he was also excited. Perhaps he got turned on by the thought of a blonde romancing with a black man.

"Yes. She was worried how her fans would take it."

"I don't think that it matters much today. There are television serials with mixed couples."

"I agree but Missy comes from another era. Now she has been putting conditions about the photo shoot with her black co-star."

"What kind of conditions?"

"This is not the right moment to go into the details but I feel that you would be the right person to see her through this crisis."

"You think that a black man like me can do the job?"

"Yes. I imagine that assigning a white person to this project may not be suitable."

"Why?"

"He or she may not be comfortable in working with a white actress who has done an interracial film of an erotic nature."

"So you figure that somebody else might have racist sentiments?"

"Perhaps that would be putting it too harshly. May be I did not express myself correctly."

"I'm listening."

"I was referring to a person's comfort zone. Frankly speaking, Annabelle would not have been suitable for this assignment."

Lisa was relieved when Jason looked convinced.

"I need somebody to be at Missy's beck and call during her entire stay. I know that you put in a lot of extra hours on the job here. We need somebody dedicated like you."

"Thanks, Mrs Donovan."

"I will be having dinner with Ms McGuire tomorrow evening and would like you to join us,"

Lisa used a tone that indicated that it was more like an order.

"I would be delighted," Jason said. She saw that he seemed to be only too happy.

"Good!" Lisa exclaimed. "I suppose that you have formal attire?"

Jason nodded but Lisa noticed that his doubtful face showed that he would probably have to hire a tuxedo.

"Meet me at this restaurant," she handed him the restaurant's visiting card. "Be there at seven sharp."

Lisa gave a sigh of relief when Jason left her office. She had found the right person for this assignment.

Chapter 12
Jason – Los Angeles 2006

Jason put on a triumphant look as he left Lisa's office. He knew that the people in the office were wondering why the CEO had called him.

He made a beeline for John's cubicle.

"Did you have a good meeting?"

John leaned forward over his table.

"Lisa has taken me off the Harry Stern project. I have to hand the papers to Annabelle."

"You've been given the new assignment," John said. "Frankly I was not expecting that it would be so soon."

John waited for Jason to say something.

"As you know, it's kind of confidential. I can't talk about it."

"OK, I get the picture."

Jason got up to leave.

"By the way, feel free to get in touch with me in case you need any help."

"Thanks."

Jason turned around and left the glass cubicle.

It was only when he was at his desk that Jason felt the excitement bubble within him. Stay cool, boy. Missy McGuire had been every black man's blonde fantasy twenty years ago. Now he was having dinner with her and another white woman. He had some research to do on Missy. If he played it right then this was a chance in a lifetime.

Annabelle came to see him.

"John told me to take over the Harry Stern contract project from you now."

She had an apologetic look.

"Here's the folder." Jason gave Annabelle a thick brown folder. "I am sure that you will be able to close the deal.".

"I hope that you aren't upset."

"No big deal." Jason smiled.

Annabelle waited for Jason to say something more and looked disappointed when he kept quiet.

Jason, eager to get on with his research, shifted his gaze to his PC monitor. Annabelle got the message and left.

Jason typed Melissa McGuire's name on the Google start page and then clicked on the links that came up. Within an hour, he had printed more than twenty pages of photos and newspaper reports. Leafing through the pages, he followed Missy's career from beauty queen to fashion model to Hollywood star to retirement in Lynchburg, Tennessee.

Missy, as a teen-aged "Miss Lynchburg", posed in a swimming costume with one hand over her hair. Eager smile, smooth bared armpit, beautiful breasts, flat belly, white thighs with her honey blonde hair tumbling down her shoulders. She looked the part of an all-American wholesome beauty.

Missy, as a New York model, photographed for a fashion magazine spread. One photo had her posturing with imploring eyes and a cigarette dangling between her teeth, one hand over the low décolleté of a short black dress with thin shoulder straps and the other one just over her knees. It was sheer erotic chic.

Missy, at the height of her film career, photographed for a film poster. The studio had remodelled her into a sex bomb with cotton-candy fine-spun platinum-blonde hair, glossy red lips and a big bosom. The change from New York model to Hollywood star was perceptible.

Missy, twenty years later, snapped at a cocktail party to promote a television series. She had a suggestive see-through costume, the back cut so low that the tops of her buttocks were visible, a cooing, sexy funny blonde doll, wriggling in front of the camera.

The latest image showed Missy, now retired in her Lynchburg home, in a red satin V-neck top, white short shorts and red satin high heeled shoes. Jason's penis stirred, as he looked carefully at the tell-tale mound between her legs. This is one hell of a sexy dame.

Jason was perplexed. Something was not adding up. Why did she suddenly leave Hollywood in the seventies? What was she doing for two decades before signing up with to do the TV series? One person who would know would be Bubba. He was a reporter with the Los Angeles Sentinel, the weekly Afro-American newspaper, and had good contacts with the film industry.

"Bubba," he asked over the telephone. "I need to talk to you about Melissa McGuire, the sex bomb who acted in 'Go for it'?"

"You are talking about Missy?" asked Bubba. "She's history. Why are you interested?"

"Our agency will be handling her arrangements in Los Angeles and I want to know more about her. I mean, you know, stuff that hasn't appeared in the press."

"You want to dig dirt?" laughed Bubba. "Let's meet for dinner at Jamal's Soul Food. You buy me some chicken wings and I'll see what I can do,"

"OK, see you there at seven."

As he drove from downtown Los Angeles to Watts, Jason felt that he was entering another world. He had inherited his grandmother's apartment after she died and his parents had moved to a safer locality in Orange County. Having been born here, he knew how to survive in this rough ghetto. Most of his best friends, including Bubba, lived close to his place and he was used to the graffiti-marked walls, abandoned carcasses of cars and boarded-up windows that were the trademark of this neighbourhood. Only the area had changed in the last decade and now there were more Latinos than blacks. Maybe if he had more money, he would also move out to Orange County.

Before going to Mamie's Soul Food, Jason purchased a tuxedo from Santa Fe Seconds. It cost just fifty dollars and the trousers were just a wee bit long. He congratulated himself on his luck.

Bubba was waiting for him at the restaurant.

"What took you so long?" He waved a bottle of Coors.

"I just bought a tuxedo," he said. The two friends conversed about clothes for a while before Bubba came to the point.

"Why are you so interested in that honky dame Missy McGuire?"

"Our agency has signed her as our client. I've doing some research on her. She left Hollywood about twenty years ago and just returned last year for a TV series. Something must have happened to cause her to leave so suddenly. Would you have any inside information?"

"Well, I have called Benny, the barman at Watts Tower," said Bubba. "The guy remembers hearing some rumours about Missy. He will be here in a while."

Benny soon appeared, a honey-coloured slim man in black T-shirt and jeans with a tooth-pick in his mouth.

"Nice to see both of you here," said Benny, as he pulled up a chair and joined their table.

After the introductions, Jason ordered a round of beers and they got to the subject of Missy McGuire.

"Sure," said Benny. "I've heard about Missy. She likes black guys."

"Do you have proof?" Jason asked.

"Folks here were talking about her and Jackson Coots," Benny replied.

"Jackson, the black welterweight champion?" asked Jason. "Who told you?"

"Jackson's trainer, Chris," Benny replied. "He used to be a regular at my bar."

"What did he tell you?"

"He said that he had seen Missy at Jackson's training camp in the Catskills. She had driven by car from New York and they had spent the weekend together."

"Is the guy for real?"

"Yes," Benny replied. "He has some Polaroids that he had taken of Missy and Jackson. They must have been taken in the seventies and were fading."

"What else did he tell you?"

"Chris said that they had a hot thing going until Missy left New York for Hollywood."

"I remember that was MG Studio signed up Missy to debut in a sex comedy."

"Chris said that Jackson used to fly to LA to be with her. Suddenly Missy dropped him. A month later he died in a drunken accident."

"Is Chris saying that Missy broke Jackson's heart?"

"Never trust a honky, Chris used to say."

"How come this affair was kept under wraps all this time?" Jason asked.

"Don't ask me," Benny replied. "The bitch was well-connected."

"What about the photos?" Jason asked.

61

"After Jackson's death, Chris says that he found the photos in Jackson's training kit," replied Benny. "Like I said, he used to pass them around in the bar. Back in those years, it was hot stuff."

"Like what? Were there any shots of Jackson fucking Missy?"

"No, nothing like that," replied Benny. "No porn, just the two embracing each other."

"Can you check with Chris?" Jason asked. "We are handling Missy's public relations and I need to know everything about her. I will make it worth your while."

"Chris is a sick man," replied Benny. "He is bedridden and living with his sister. I could go and see him."

"Can you get those photos from him?"

"Sure, but it will cost you something. He is broke and has unpaid doctor's bills. I would say that he will part with the photos for five hundred bucks."

"Make it three hundred. There will be hundred for you," offered Jason. "Bubba will see you at the bar tomorrow and bring them across to me."

Benny just shrugged. Jason was not sure whether he meant yes or no. He would use his credit card to buy the chicken wings for everybody and hope that Bubba would be able to work out a deal with Benny later.

Jason was excited. He was on to something and his research was on the fast track.

They parted company and Jason drove to his home.

***   ***   *** *** ***

Jason had just showered and tried out his second-hand tuxedo when Bubba turned up in his apartment.

"I've got the photos from Benny," he announced grandly, his right hand waving a bunch of Polaroid shots. "You owe me two hundred bucks."

Jason grabbed the dog-eared prints from Bubba and the two sat on the couch to view them together. The colours were fading but the pictures clearly showed a blonde woman and a black man together. Jason recognised the woman as Missy and surmised that the black man was Jackson Coots, the boxer.

62

The photos were apparently taken in the countryside against a backdrop of trees or fields. Most showed the two together either hand-in-hand or embracing each other. Two shots showed them kissing each other. One was sitting on a bench and the other standing against a tree. There was a pornographic quality about the well-thumbed photos, as if they had been furtively passed from hand to hand.

"Man, this is dynamite," exclaimed Jason. "How did the studio manage to keep this stuff under wraps at that time?"

"I did some investigating and it's a long story."

Bubba went on to explain that the studio was concerned about any negative backlash concerning Missy's affair with Jackson since it was distributing her latest movie 'Go for it'. If the news about her affair with a black boxer became public then that the South could have boycotted the film. The studio's PR boys paid off the journalists. It was rumoured that the studio head had called in the mob to put the pressure on Jackson and his manager, Eddie Conklin. Amidst this storm, probably Missy decided to quit the Hollywood scene until everything cooled down.

"The photos will be strictly for your personal use," Bubba said. "Nothing will be posted on the web. Jackson is still a hero for many brothers."

"I promise," replied Jason.

"Where are the three hundred bucks?" asked Bubba, holding out his hand.

"I'm rather tight now. Take hundred and I'll settle the rest by the end of next week."

Jason shoved Bubba toward the door. Bubba turned around.

"Don't push me. Just get the dough by next Friday."

"Okay."

"By the way, don't jack off on those images. We all know about your thing for white women. Remember that weekend in Las Vegas?"

"Get out of here," Jason shouted, pushing Bubba out of the door.

Tonight opportunity beckoned and it would be up to him to seize the initiative.

Jason grew excited just thinking about his encounter with Liz in Las Vegas. It still provided the fuel for his masturbatory experiences. He was hooked on older white women and Liz served as his ideal. Yet, he never found another woman to match his experience with Liz. The white strippers in bars catering to black men were brash, loud and vulgar. He was just another black man willing to pay for white gash. No, Jason knew that he wanted something better, something classy.

Jason had to concede that he was one of those black men who thought that white women were sexier. He wondered how his evening with two ravishing white women would play out.

Chapter 13
Jason – Los Angeles 2006

"Have you reserved a table?" The door attendant at the sidewalk gate on Robertson Boulevard looked suspiciously at Jason.

At 7 pm, Jason, standing outside the gourmet restaurant, was irritated at the man's haughty behaviour.

"I have an appointment with Ms Liza Cummins. She has reserved a table for three."

The door attendant beckoned to the tuxedoed headwaiter. "This gentleman is for the Cummins' table."

The headwaiter led him through the ornate dining room into an open patio lit up with lamps. There were more than forty tables occupied by people dining. As he followed the waiter to a far corner, there was a low buzz of conversation and the clatter of crockery. He sighted Lisa, already seated with an attractive blonde woman on a round table laid out for three.

"Hello Jason. You're bang on time." Lisa looked at her small square watch.

"Please meet Melissa McGuire."

Jason saw a striking, lush-bodied blonde, just a little past the prime of her physical beauty. She was dressed for summer with a white halter top sundress, barely covering her knees. Her legs were bare and she had high heel open-toe white shoes.

He held out his hand to the seated woman.

"Good evening Ms McGuire. I'm Jason Grant."

Jason noticed the woman's large blue eyes show a flicker of interest.

"Jason handles our relations with our key clients," said Lisa, "He is there to make your stay in Los Angeles comfortable. Please do not hesitate to call upon his services should you need anything."

"Anything?" The blonde smiled.

It could have been intended as a suggestive remark but Jason could see that she was only acting. Yet, he hoped that her question was intended as an innuendo for services of a sexual nature.

The thought excited Jason. He felt a stirring in his groin, his senses assailed by the odour of her intoxicating perfume, the sight of her smooth white legs and the sound of her sulphurous voice.

Lisa laughed uneasily. "Well, you ask him," she replied.

"Jason," said Missy, looking him in the eye, "I'm sure that Lisa has selected you with the certainty that you will be able to handle any of my requests."

"I'll try my best," said Jason.

Jason quickly looked away from her questioning blue eyes and placed a hand over the crotch of his trousers. He felt Missy looking at him as if she understood the reason for his discomfort.

"Jason," Lisa said. "Your welcome glass of champagne is waiting for you."

Jason noticed a waiter with a glass on a tray.

"I didn't order any champagne,"

Lisa laughed.

"It is on the house. Every guest gets a complimentary glass of French fizz."

Jason took the glass, slightly embarrassed at being unaware that this restaurant offered free champagne.

The two women raised their glasses.

"Here's to a successful stay in Los Angeles," Lisa said. The three glasses clinked.

"You can count on me for anything, Ms McGuire,"

"Thank you, Jason. Just call me Missy. Everybody does."

Jason looked at Lisa. She nodded reassuringly.

"It's alright. Missy is an informal person."

Jason took his first ever gulp of champagne, experiencing a heady sensation. He noticed people at a nearby table looking at them. A woman whispered something in a man's ear and the man took out a pair of spectacles.

Jason wondered whether they were looking at Missy, since celebrities usually ate at such restaurants.

The sight of two mature white women in the company of a young black man was certainly intriguing in such a chic restaurant. Perhaps they looked like two white cougars on the prowl for sexual adventures with a black panther. The very thought excited him.

When the waiter came to take their orders, Lisa insisted that Jason order a sixteen ounce Kobe-style New York steak. It was the

66

most expensive item on the menu. The women passed up on starters and ordered lobster ravioli.

The two women resumed their earlier conversation about life in Los Angeles, oblivious to the stir they were causing around them. Jason did not participate in the discussion but looked at each woman when she talked. He gave the polite impression that he was being attentive to their banter. At the same time, he was observing them carefully.

Jason played out his fantasies about the two women.

He imagined Lisa, with her neck-length silver-blue hair and black cocktail dress, as a successful executive whose cool reserve concealed a fiery temperament.

On the other hand, Missy, in her short summer dress, had the look of a matron on holiday seeking an exotic sexual adventure. Did she travel to Jamaica to satisfy her penchant for black men?

Jason wondered if Missy went for younger men. He had read that women past their menopause had an increased sexual drive. Missy fitted in this category. He noticed signs of her maturity: marks on her throat, faint liver spots on her hands, a slight rounding of the stomach and a slight padding around her hips. Jason thought that for a woman of around sixty, she was still in reasonably good shape.

Jason's musings were disturbed when Missy suddenly stretched out, pushed her chair back and turned towards Jason to cross her legs. For an instant, Jason saw her smooth shaven white legs come apart to reveal a white thong with a shadow on the crotch. Did this blonde bleach her bush? Missy legs stayed slightly apart and Jason could not keep his eyes off her exposed white thighs. Was this woman a cock-teaser, putting on a show? Or was she just unconsciously stretching her legs for a short while?

Jason's thoughts went back to the photos. He imagined the clandestine trysts between this blonde actress and her black lover. What did they do when they were alone together? Did she suck his black cock? Did he fuck her in a doggy position? Try as he could, Jason could not get these thoughts out of his head.

Jason's thoughts were interrupted when dinner was served. It surpassed his expectations.

The steak, thick as his wrist and tender, melted in his mouth like cotton candy. Lisa and Missy seemed to be happy with their lobster and pasta dish.

They had switched from champagne to a bottle of French Pouilly-Fumé and Jason shared a glass of white wine with them. He had not dared to order a bottle of beer in this swank restaurant.

Missy spoke little and ate slowly. Often she lifted her fork to her lips and then lowered it, as she listened to Lisa's stories. Jason observed that her mind seemed to be somewhere else. It looked as if she was trying hard to be a good guest.

The women skipped dessert and ordered double espressos. Jason followed suit.

It was during coffee that Missy spoke up.

"I'm not comfortable with the final version of the film and am reluctant to do the photo shoot."

She was cool and composed but had a determined look.

"I thought that it was all settled," Lisa protested.

"No, everything is still open. I signed the contract on the premise that we would be doing a tasteful film with an interracial romance theme. Instead, I've been conned into doing a soft porn feature. I'm really not comfortable with this release because I thought that we're doing an art film. Instead, I've landed in a sex exploitation film and am having second thoughts about it."

"We've already arranged the photo shoot for tomorrow," reasoned Lisa. "Sleep over it tonight and let's meet at the Alexander's studio to talk it over."

"I reserve the right to back out unless we agree to do some cuts in the film."

"Whatever you want," replied Lisa. "I want you to be in your comfort zone but let's discuss it tomorrow."

Lisa smiled to break the tension but Missy had a look of quiet determination. There was a quiet pause when both women faced each other for a minute.

Missy suddenly got up. "I need to freshen up."

As soon as she was gone, Lisa Cummins leaned close to Jason. "Can you drop Missy at the Beverly Hills Hotel in your car?"

"I've just got a Hyundai compact. Are you sure that Missy will be comfortable?"

"I've let Missy's limousine go and I'll be calling for a cab to get back to my place."

"Are you sure that it is alright? I mean, me, a black guy, driving with a white woman at this time of the night? Are you sure that Missy won't mind?"

"Jason! We're in the twenty-first century." Lisa sighed. "Missy doesn't give a damn about your colour. All she needs is to be dropped back at her hotel as soon as possible."

"She seems to be upset."

"This is where you come in. You have to make sure that she gets to Alexander's studio on time tomorrow. Until then your job is to take care of all her requests. Missy is a star and used to getting royal treatment. If she wants a bottle of Dom Perignon champagne, make sure that the hotel concierge gets it. If she wants some white stuff to get high, you know where to look for it. All I'm asking you to do is to chaperon her and make sure that she is in a good mood when you bring her to the studio tomorrow."

"So I drop her tonight at the hotel and pick her up tomorrow morning and drive her to Alexander's Studio?"

"Yes, you've got it right."

When Missy returned, she was in a lighter mood. When Lisa informed her that Jason would be driving her to the hotel, she pretended to swoon and her eyes fluttered dreamily. Jason saw that she could change personalities in a New York minute.

"You do know how to take care of an old lady?" Missy gave him a pleading smile.

Jason nodded. His thoughts went back to the photos. The woman in those photos was standing in flesh-and-blood before him. If he played his cards right, she might even open up to him. There was much at stake and his job depended on keeping her in a good mood.

Chapter 14
Missy – Los Angeles 2006

After saying good-bye to Lisa, Missy accompanied Jason to the parking lot. When he located his car, she saw that it was a battered Hyundai Accent.

Rather than being disappointed, Missy was relieved. She had assumed that this young hulk of a man would be driving a sports car, perhaps even a Porsche. In a way, she felt more comfortable getting into a compact rather than a low-seated racing machine. She hopped into the passenger's seat.

"Do you know the way to the Beverley Hilton?"

Missy observed Jason's profile, as he was reversing the car. She found that his straight nose and prominent chin gave him the look of a Nubian warrior.

"Sure, I've been coming to this area quite often."

Once Jason drove into the main boulevard, Missy questioned him about his life in Los Angeles. She found him to be quite forthcoming. He was no longer the reserved man she had encountered at dinner.

Missy soon picked up quite a bit of information about Jason's parents, his schooling, his college days as a basketball star and his present job.

While talking, Missy noticed that Jason was sneaking looks at her exposed white knees. Although her dress had ridden way up to her thighs, she decided to leave it that way. In a way, she had always been a bit of a cock teaser.

After her questioning had stopped, there was silence for a few minutes. Missy looked at Jason and saw that he was looking a bit uncomfortable.

"Is everything alright?"

Jason opened his mouth to say something and then suddenly stopped

"Is there anything that you want to say? Be go ahead. Don't be shy."

Missy patted his lap comfortingly, withdrawing suddenly when she sensed his erection.

Jason took a deep breath. "Mrs McGuire, can I ask you a personal question?"

"Jason, I've already told you once before. Please call me Missy. Everybody does."

"Missy, this is a purely personal question," Jason explained. "Please don't be offended."

"Go ahead."

"Is it true that you were involved with Jackson Coots?"

Missy stiffened and her heart beat faster.

"Why are you asking?"

"Well, I happened to see some photos of Jackson and you today," Jason explained. "There are old Polaroid shots taken years ago."

Missy felt frightened and angry at the same time. This black man, who earlier seemed so likeable, now took on a menacing role. Obviously he had been digging up on her past.

"How did you get them?" Missy asked. "Do you have them with you?"

"Yes. One of my friends got them from Jackson's trainer, Chris."

Missy's mind went back to the fateful Sunday morning some thirty years ago when Chris had taken those Polaroid shots of Jackson and her. For years, she wanted to lay her hands on them.

"Can I see them?"

"Sure but I'd like to get your version about your involvement with Jackson," replied Jason. "Some folks are saying that Jackson took to drink because of you."

Missy was offended. First this man claimed to have seen some photographs of her with Jackson. Now he was blaming her for Jackson's alcoholism.

"Young man, I don't appreciate you prying into my private life. Are you trying to blackmail me? Did Lisa put you up to it?"

"No, let me explain."

"Please stop the car. I want to get out."

Missy wanted to just get away from this man and his inquisition. She put her hand on the door handle.

"No, Missy, don't get me wrong. I just want to know what happened and you will get the photos. That will be the end of the affair."

71

"Please stop the car at once."

Missy banged her hand against Jason's shoulder. She noticed that they were driving through a secluded wooded area but she did not care about being alone on the road at this time of the night.

Reluctantly Jason stopped the car. "Please don't get out. Let me explain."

Missy got out, banging the car door behind her. She walked briskly, her high heels clacking sharply on the concrete sidewalk. Suddenly she tripped when a shoe stiletto plunged into a hole and was falling when she felt Jason holding her arm to steady her.

"Let me go."

Missy shook herself free. She continued walking with Jason two steps behind her, pleading with her to listen to him.

"Missy, please just hear me out. Let's talk for a minute."

Missy stopped. She was breathless and her shoes were pinching her. She turned around to face Jason.

"Did Lisa put you up to this piece of blackmail?"

"Lisa has nothing to do with this," protested Jason. "Please listen to me. I had obtained those photos on my own initiative because I was curious of your past. Don't be mad at me. You'll get your photos back."

Missy felt her initial anger and panic was subsiding.

"Alright, I believe you," whispered Missy. "Where are the photos?"

"They are in the glove compartment of the car."

Missy was relieved. The boy had probably worked on his own initiative and she could talk him into getting those photos back.

"Those photos are from a chapter from my life that I have been trying to put behind me."

"Perhaps it'll help if you tell me about it, I mean people think that Jackson killed himself because of you and we need your version."

Missy decided that a little talk might help in settling the matter.

"It's a long story. Let's sit for a while on that bench. We have been a long while in that restaurant and I need some fresh air."

Missy led the way towards a bench with a panoramic view of Los Angeles. A row of trees hid the bench from the main path.

"This is nice but do you think that's a good idea?" Jason looked around.

"The view is great." Missy patted the place beside her on the bench.

Jason sat on the bench, a little away from her. He looked around.

"Cops normally patrol this area."

"We're only chatting on a bench and just enjoying the fresh air".

"They might get nasty if they see a black man with a white woman. I'm not looking for that kind of trouble."

"You might get into worse trouble if I don't get those photos."

"I promise that you'll get them when we go back to the car."

"I thought that those photos no longer existed. You must tell me how you got them."

Jason explained how his friend, Bubba, had helped him to obtain the photos.

Although irritated about Jason's investigations into her sex life, Missy was relieved that he had succeeded in finding the photos. They would be out of circulation once she got them..

"How many Polaroids do you have?"

"Ten."

"I remember that I wasn't comfortable when Jackson's trainer took those pictures."

"You probably didn't think that those Polaroids would last for so long."

"I can only remember Jackson insisting on embracing or kissing me in various poses."

"They are pretty harmless by today's standards."

"I suppose that he wanted them as souvenirs of our weekend together but they got into the wrong hands."

"It looks as if that is what happened."

"Back in those days, such photos were dynamite. Confidential Magazine caused a stir when they printed photos of Ava Gardner with Sammy Davis Junior."

"It didn't do any harm to Ava's career."

"Remember, she was still with Frank. She rode out that storm. Sammy wasn't so lucky."

"What happened?"

73

"Columbia Studio threatened to have him beaten up after he got involved with Kim Novak. They almost married."

"That's strange. Black stars from that era like Harry Belafonte and Sidney Poitier have white wives too."

"They were low key. A newspaperman lost his job for printing a photo of Sugar Ray Robinson in his dancing clothes surrounded by a dozen white chorus girls."

"Sugar was a great boxer."

"I know but black and white didn't mix in public in those days."

Missy was enjoying reminiscing about Hollywood's strict code concerning interracial relationships. They talked about the sexual mores in the sixties for a few more minutes. She felt that this young black man should appreciate the fact that he was living in more liberal times.

Missy placed her hand on Jason's thigh. Sensing Jason's erection again, she hastily raised her hand and noticed her bracelet gleaming in the moonlight.

Preferring to ignore Jason's sexual state, she changed the subject.

"It's full moon."

Jason looked upwards and then admiringly at her hair.

"Your hair looks straw white in the moon beams. This is pure magic."

Jason looked as if he was about to touch her hair and she was moved by his admiration for her blonde hair. Luckily it was dark and he could not see the ageing wrinkles on her neck.

"I've answered your questions. Are you ready to answer a few of mine?"

Missy saw Jason's pleading brown eyes moving towards her. She felt a familiar throb between her legs but maintained a calm posture.

"OK, go ahead."

"Missy, some brothers in Watts think that you had something going on with Jackson. Me, I just want to know the truth about Jackson and you."

"What is your question?"

"How did you meet Jackson?"

"Eddie Conklin, Jackson's manager, introduced me to Jackson in Las Vegas. Eddie came over to me just as I was leaving the roulette table at the Casino Royale after a losing streak."

Missy brushed a strand of hair from her forehead.

"Are we talking about the same Eddie who set up the fight between Jackson and Billy Meyers in Las Vegas?"

Missy felt Jason edging closer towards her. She was glad to feel his warmth and take in a waft of his after-shave lotion.

"Yes. I first met Eddie when I was working as a photo model in a studio in Los Angeles.

"Your biography makes no mention about your stint as a photo model in Los Angeles."

"Photo model may not be the right word. After leaving Lynchburg, I found it difficult to find a acting job in Hollywood and ended up working in a dubious photo studio."

Missy hesitated for a minute and then decided to continue.

"You know the kind of place where men had one-on-one photo sessions with female models. We would be topless and sometimes even nude but the men were not allowed to touch us."

"Were all the models white?"

"Yes but we did have black customers. Eddie was among the regular black customers who came to the studio. He had two expensive cameras, just took a few photos and talked a lot. I think that was the time when he was a pimp, looking for white girls for his stable. Anyway, Eddie and I became quite friendly but he never propositioned me. So I was happy to see him when he turned up in Las Vegas."

"I didn't know that you started as a nude model," exclaimed Jason. "As a Southern woman, how did you feel about posing in the nude before black men?"

"In the beginning, I was uncomfortable. Remember, I grew up in Lynchburg where there were hardly any black people. My first black client was an old man who talked a lot. He made me feel good and at ease."

"I suppose in those times such photo studios were places where black men could link up with white women."

"Sure but most black men for photo sessions behaved just like white men. They wanted sexy crotch shots for their private collections. Only one or two touched themselves after a few camera shots. It wasn't allowed but nobody cared. In fact, the manager liked black repeat customers. They were good for the business and some also tipped well."

"It must have been quite an experience for somebody from the South."

"Yes and it was my first experience close up with black men. No physical contact but they were polite even after they shot their loads. No, black men always treated me well."

"Did your family know what you were doing?" Jason asked.

"Oh, goodness, no," exclaimed Missy, "I had to start somewhere and needed the money to pay my rent. The men would ask me to pose and I learned to do it right so that they got their shots. As a matter of fact, I was particularly nice to black clients because I felt that they were getting a raw deal in the outside world. I was nice to them and they appreciated being treated with respect by a white woman. It was reciprocal and an attraction of opposites."

"So you are aware that certain black men are attracted to white women?"

"Yeah and it is a kind of turn-on for me to know that black men were turned on by my blonde beauty," replied Missy.

"You are still very beautiful," said Jason tenderly.

"Why thank you Jason. That's very nice of you to say. Let me get back to how I met Jackson." Missy paused to gather her breath. "After some small talk, Eddie told me that he was in Las Vegas to manage Jackson's fight with Billy Meyers."

"Was it the time when Jackson knocked out Billy in Las Vegas?"

"Yeah, it was that fight," Missy replied. "Eddie said that Jackson was from Harlem and never had a white woman. He made a proposal that I should take care of Jackson and he would pay me for it. I asked if he thought that I was a hooker and he thought that I could use the money since he had seen that I had lost a pile at the roulette table."

"Did Eddie's pitch bother you?" Jason asked.

"No, it didn't," replied Missy. "I'd always suspected that Eddie was a pimp who procured white women for black men. He wasn't really pimping for Jackson but just wanted to reward him for winning. The irony of ironies was that Eddie's offer was a

76

solution to my immediate problems. I needed the money to cover my expenses until I was back to Los Angeles."

Jason leaned forward and asked, "Goodness, don't tell me that you accepted Eddie's offer to sleep with Jackson?" His voice tingled with excitement.

"Well, I asked Eddie how much was he going to offer me and what did he expect me to do."

"How did it go?"

"Eddie offered me most of what I had lost," replied Missy. "It was a thousand dollars for less than an hour's work".

"Wow," exclaimed Jason.

"In a way, I was flattered," said Missy. "I was not exactly a spring chicken and Jackson was younger than me. I am sure that many white women would have given anything to sleep with Jackson. He was a champion and looked a known ladies' man. Eddie's proposal had aroused my curiosity about Jackson."

"What happened next?" Missy sensed Jason's excitement, almost as a voyeur in a peep show.

Missy simply smiled and looked at Jason. She placed his hand on his thigh, moving higher till it just stopped short of the hard muscle trapped in his underwear.

"Eddie made a phone call and told me that Jackson would be down in ten minutes," Missy said. "He suggested that we meet him outside the hotel."

"How did it go?"

"When I saw Jackson striding towards us, he looked like a black panther making his way through the jungle. I thought that he was beautiful."

Missy stopped for a minute and then continued. "Jackson was shy and our conversation was brief. Eddie slipped him a piece of paper with my room number and he politely took his leave. Eddie was as good as his word and passed me a bundle of bills just as we parted company."

"That was pretty neat," exclaimed Jason.

"Back in my room, I took a shower to calm my nerves," Missy said. "I was shaking while waiting for the expected phone call. When the phone did ring, I jumped and picked it up at the first ring."

"It was Jackson and he asked whether he could come in half-an-hour," Missy continued. "He asked me to leave my room door slightly ajar."

Jason' heart was pounding. He was impatient for Missy to continue.

"After showering, I added touches of perfume all over my body and slipped on a pink negligee set," Missy said. "I was on a holiday and didn't even have stockings."

"Jackson was shy in the beginning. He started talking when I asked him questions about his childhood." Missy continued,

"I knew that he was overawed in being in the presence of a photo model and we sat on the bed and had some wine to break the ice. When I kissed him, it was a nice sweet kiss but I felt his tongue on my lips and opened my mouth. After our deep kiss, I pulled the dress down my shoulders and Jackson helped me slide it down my body. He gasped when he saw that I just had my garter belt and stockings and undressed quickly. I lay on the bed while he took off his clothes. He had the rock hard body of a boxer and he entered me with little foreplay. It was over in five minutes. After that he kept on repeating that I was beautiful."

"What happened next?"

"After returning to Los Angeles, my luck changed for the better. Eddie would set me up from time to time with a fancy black client and pay me well."

"Eddie was pimping for you?"

"Once you've crossed over, like taking money from a man for sex, you can't go back to what you've been. The money was good and I started investing in clothes and treating myself to health spas. Eventually I decided to get out of the nude model business. Eddie introduced me to Dave Gosner, the fashion photographer, and we did publicity shots for swimsuit brands. Dave hired me and I relocated to the Big Apple."

"I remember reading about your modelling stint for Matchless Cosmetics."

"Dave got a two-year contract from Matchless and I became Miss Matchless. Dave and I shared the same apartment but he was hopelessly gay and would have his pretty boy over for the weekends. It was about the time when Jackson was training for his fights in the Catskills Mountains and he got in touch with me, asking if I could spend the weekends with him."

"I suppose the photos were taken near his training camp?"

"Yes, they were taken by his trainer. I wasn't too keen but Jackson insisted. I didn't realise that the photos would end up being circulated in Watts. For heaven's sake, I don't want them on the net."

"You'll get them once I drop you at the hotel," replied Jason. "Why did you break up with Jackson?"

Missy sighed.

"Our relationship lasted for a few years. We would meet now and then over the weekends. Jackson was a tireless lover and the sex relaxed me. I was too busy to have an emotional relationship with anybody else until I met Greg, my late husband, years later."

"It must have been a great experience for Jackson." Jason exclaimed. He was now really excited, as he visualised the interracial encounter in his mind's eye. Like Jason, Jackson had been jet black and the contrast in the skin colours between the black boxer and white movie star turned Jason on. Missy's hand was inching towards his involuntary erection. Did she realise that her talk was exciting him?

"Unfortunately, our affair was doomed. I knew that it couldn't last. When MG Studios offered me a bit part in one of their films, I returned to Hollywood. I was wanted to focus on my film career and forget about Jackson for a while. I knew that he wanted to marry me and he even came to the West Coast to plead with me."

"The studio got wind of our affair," Missy continued. "Martin Grover, the studio head, called me and told me to stop seeing Jackson. He called the mob to warn Eddie Conklin about Jackson. The mob even threatened to beat up Jackson if he did not leave me alone. It was just too much. Jackson left Los Angeles without saying good-bye. I knew that he was heart-broken. He had loved me like nobody else but it would have never worked out for us."

"Didn't you feel bad about Jackson? He started drinking and then got killed in that horrible car accident."

"Why, of course!" Missy replied. "I still miss Jackson after all these years. Apart from Greg, he was really the only man who really loved me. Now that I think about it, you remind me of him."

Missy moved her hand closer to his crotch. She felt his erection. The recital of her affair with Jackson had stirred old memories and excited her too.

"Missy, you're a woman with a heart." Missy felt Jason move closer towards her.

Missy did not resist. She put her arms around Jason's neck, pulling him towards her. They kissed. She opened her mouth slightly and their tongue tips touched each other. They lay entwined in a passionate embrace. For all his youth, Jason was a seasoned kisser. Apart from basketball, he must have picked up a number of other pointers during his college days.

"You're as sweet as Jackson," Missy murmured, stroking his short curly hair. "Be kind to me."

Jason fingers fumbled with the halter top knot behind her neck. Missy quickly reached to help him. Once the knot was untied, Jason eased down the halter top to expose the rounded softness of Missy's breasts. She gasped when he placed a circle of kisses around the edge of the puffy aureole before pulling the hard knob of nipple deep in his mouth. His tongue pressed it against the roof of his mouth, softly at first, then demanding more, sucking on it with a passionate intensity. Missy writhed and wrapped her arms around him.

"I want to go down on you," pleaded Jason.

"No," warned Missy. "Not here."

Jason did not listen to her plea. Instead she felt him pulling up her skirt. Involuntarily she moaned and spread her legs. She felt him pushing aside her thong and kneeling between her legs.

Missy closed her eyes, imagining his dark head framed between her milky white thighs.

Jason was now scattering quick kisses over the slight, womanly roundness of her tummy. Effortlessly lifting Missy's hips, Jason dived forward, burying his hungry mouth in the soft, moist centre of her femininity.

Jason's tongue parted the soft lips, searching for the sensitive seat of her pleasure and teasing it. His lips closed gently around the tiny stem and tugged gently before sucking on it.

Missy's back arched at the pleasure. He redoubled his efforts by lapping the length of her vaginal lips. His tongue sank deeper to slurp down her earthy juices. His tensing fingers dug into the creamy globes of Missy's hips as his lips and tongue combined to drive her to ecstasy. Missy stifled a cry and her hips arched against Jason's mouth. She shook in the throes of explosive release.

In the distance, they heard the sound of a car coming their way. Quickly he got up while Missy arranged her thong and got up to smoothen down her dress.

They stood behind a tree while a Beverly Hills police car passed them. It had been a close shave.

Missy could not get over what had happened. Not since Jackson had another black man brought her to such as explosive orgasm.

As they walked towards Jason's car, she wanted the magic spell of this evening to continue into the night.

Chapter 15
Missy – Los Angeles 2006

"Would you like to join me for a nightcap?"

Missy asked Jason when he arrived at the Beverly Hills Hilton. She did not want their time together to end.

"That would be great,"

"Park your car and join me at the Governor's suite on the top floor. Don't forget to bring the photos."

Jason nodded.

As she got out of the Hyundai, the doorman recognized Missy and tipped his cap.

"Welcome back, Ms McGuire."

If he was shocked that Missy was in the company of a black man, he was discrete enough not to show it.

The young man at the front desk also recognized Missy.

"Is there anything we can do to make your stay more comfortable?"

"No thank you."

Missy felt the dampness between her legs. She needed to get out of her panties before Jason arrived.

Once she entered the eighth floor Governor's Suite, she stripped off her frock and underwear in the bedroom and moved to the dressing room to put on a white bath robe.

A few minutes later, there was a knock on the door. Missy let Jason in. He looked surprised to see her in a bathrobe.

"I thought that I would get into something more comfortable."

"I think that I'll strip too."

Jason looked around and she could see that he was impressed with the large living room, which included a brown leather sofa set and a round conference table.

"Wow, this is something."

Jason placed his jacket over a chair and took off his bow tie.

"The studio arranged this."

"It must have cost a fortune."

"It's in their marketing budget."

Jason looked around and even peaked into the bedroom.

"Mind if I use your bathroom?"

"Be my guest."

Missy assumed that he wanted to wash his mouth and remove the taste of her pussy juices. Nobody had gone down on her for quite a while. What a pity that they had to interrupt their sexual tryst.

"There is a guest tooth brush and a pair of cotton slippers in case your shoes are pinching you."

"Thanks, Missy."

Jason disappeared for a while and came out with his face freshened.

"Would you care for a glass of champagne?" Missy asked. She picked out a bottle from the bar, giving it to Jason to open.

Missy noticed Jason fiddling a long time with the wiring that held the cork in the bottle. She placed two slender glasses on a round table. Jason managed to open the bottle without spilling any of the bubbly on the brown carpeting. and carefully top up the glasses.

Missy was struck by the similarity between Jason and Jackson. Jason was taller but Jackson had the heavy set body of a boxer. Why was she getting involved with black men? It was true that she first slept with Jackson because she needed the money. Still he had loved her like no other man. Now several decades later she was with another black man who seemed to appreciate her white beauty or what was left of it.

"Would you like to see a panoramic view of Century City?"

Missy opened the door to the balcony. Coming out from the air-conditioned room, she enjoyed the fresh breeze blowing against her face.

Jason followed her with the two glasses. He handed Missy her drink and they clinked glasses.

"Here's to your stay in Los Angeles."

"Thanks, Jason. I'm happy to be back in this city."

"Look at the lights. This city never sleeps."

"Yes, it is exciting."

Missy felt excited but she decided to keep a lid on her emotions.

"Jason, we need to discuss our plan for tomorrow. Can we go inside?"

They walked into the living room and Missy sat on one end of a large leather sofa. Jason joined her, sitting a little away.

"Lisa told me that I've to be here at nine tomorrow to drive you to Alexander's Studio," Jason said.

"You know that I am having second thoughts about tomorrow's photo shoot?"

"Why?"

"Did Lisa tell you about the nature of the photo shoot?"

"No," Jason replied. "She only said that there would be working with a male model."

"The male model happens to be Richard Collins."

Jason gasped. Richard Collins was a black movie star, well into his fifties but highly considered in the industry.

"It was my way of coming out of the closet," said Missy. "After Jackson and I broke up, I kept away from black men. It wasn't right but I wanted to erase that chapter from my life."

"I can understand your feelings."

"When Richard's agent got in touch with me with a movie proposal, I thought about it and agreed. It was an opportunity for an ageing actress like me. The idea of doing a movie with an interracial romance theme appealed to me,"

Missy explained that she had accepted to do the film because she felt that it dealt with a controversial subject in a tasteful manner. It featured two senior actors and promoted the theme that sexuality knew no age or colour bars. In the meantime, the film had been shot in Toronto and there had been tight security. Now the photo shoot was taking place for the advance publicity.

"This is great," said Jason. "I mean that you've had the courage to act in an interracial romance with a black actor. Times have indeed changed."

"Yes, Jason, we have changed. Our films, our music, everything has changed," agreed Missy. "We can now discuss race relations but Hollywood is not ready for romance in interracial relationships."

"I'm not so sure."

"I'm talking about romance, not interracial porn. There is a lot of that stuff on the Internet."

Missy noted that Jason looked embarrassed. He probably knew what she meant.

"Richard was cast because he is a macho type. The film director focused less on the romance angle and more on the sex side. I've ended up acting in a soft porn feature. It had nothing to do with romance. We were simulating sex acts for voyeurs of interracial fantasies."

"Larry is a talented director. The feature is being marketed as an art film."

"They are calling it an art film? It's more like a senior citizen porn feature. My film career is in a state of decay."

"You are not in decay" Jason kissed her on the cheek.

"I am sixty odd years old, Jason" Missy said laughing," I am pretty much in decay."

"No. You are true beauty. Wonderful for me"

"I remind you of those old movie stars, is that it?"

"You are a classy lady. Everything is right. The way you move, your hair and your cheekbones and your eyes."

He kissed her cheek and put his arms protectively around her.

"You are my Matchless Cosmetics girl," he whispered.

Missy sighed. "Don't tell me that those ads still appear in the magazines? Those photos were taken five years ago."

This time their lips touched.

"Do I remind you of Lisa Donovan?"

Missy narrowed her eyes. They were twinkling with mischief.

"Maybe a little bit!" Jason said. He smiled.

"What about the photos?" Missy asked. "Can I have them? You promised."

Jason looked for his coat, dug into the inside pocket to pull out the photos. He handed them over to Missy. She looked at them and her eyes moistened again.

"You remind me of Jackson." Missy touched Jason's face tenderly.

She let the top of her bathrobe open a bit.

"That's a compliment. Jackson was a professional boxer and I'm just played college basketball."

"You're black and beautiful and tender like him," Missy said.

Missy spread her legs and her bath robe slipped to expose an expanse of white thigh.

"I want to make love to you," Jason said.

"Do you have a condom?"

"No," replied Jason. "But I have always made love with a condom. Believe me, I'm safe."

"Famous last words," sighed Missy.

"Alright, let me taste you once again," pleaded Jason. He moved between her legs.

Missy lay back, thinking that it was shameless the way she had opened her legs to a man young enough to be her grandson. She looked down on his black head locked between her white thighs, hoping that he would not stop.

Jason started nuzzling her inner thighs. He moved his head back to observe her flaxen muff. It was downy, trimmed short. She had often thought of being completely shaved but that would have been like a waste of her natural blonde attributes.

"You're a true blonde," Jason observed. He looked up. Missy smiled.

Jason pressed his face between her legs and his tongue was now licking the entire length of her inner lips. When Missy opened her legs a little wider, he dug his tongue into her wet depths, lapping up her juices.

Missy dug her hands into his skull until he withdrew for a breather.

"You have a taste of the sea and oysters."

"You're the first one to tell me that."

Jason went back to admire the view.

"You've a beautiful pussy."

"Stop it."

"Your clitoris has the look of a miniature cherry."

Missy had always been self-conscious of her prominent clitoris, which took on the appearance of a miniature penis when erect. Now somebody was actually praising it.

Jason lightly licked her clitoris.

"Yes, tease my clit."

Missy was shocked when the words slipped out of her mouth.

Jason increased the cadence of his licking, even lightly nibbling it.

Missy almost screamed, raising her hips. She then held his head pressed between her legs until her spasms ceased.

For a while, she luxuriated in the afterglow of her orgasm while she caressed Jason's head, lying close to her fuzzy mound.

"I want to make love to you."

Missy felt that Jason sounded almost like Jackson. She was satiated but her sex ached. She needed to be filled, to have Jason thrust inside her until she came. That is how it had been with Jackson.

Jason had given her a terrific orgasm and she owed him one. She undid the knot of her robe, letting it drop to her hips.

Missy then lay back on the sofa and pulled Jason by his shoulders on to her breast. He began sucking one of the tits and she started moaning, running her hands through his hair.

Jason moved up and they kissed. Missy felt the taste of her sex on his lips but she did not care. She pushed her tongue in his mouth and rolled it around. She could sense him gardening and was excited by his musky masculine odour.

"Come to bed," she whispered.

Jason followed her, taking off his clothes on the way. By the time that he was naked, she was already on her back on the bed, her legs apart. The bedroom was dark but the French windows to the balcony were open. In the moonlight, her platinum hair glowed like phosphorescence. Her figure, pale like a porcelain mannequin, looked seemingly fragile.

As Jason got on the bed, Missy heard his knees slip on the smooth satin sheets. When he hovered over her, she noticed that his big brown eyes now had a lustful look. Jackson sometimes had the same look when he mounted her. She felt as if she could see right into Jason's mind and understand his urge. It was the need of a black man to pound a white woman.

"Jason," she murmured. "Go easy, I haven't had a man for a long time."

Missy did not care if Jason made love without a condom. It was too late anyway.

She felt Jason go in slowly, very slowly. Gently, slowly, as if she were a virgin, he eased forward into her, the great hard knob of his erection spreading and stretching and filling her warm softness with his desire until they were one.

Now Jason increased his strokes. He became forceful. He pounded her with intensity.

Jason's animal urgency frightened her at first and then it excited her. She felt like a white sex goddess to have him desire her with such wild and wanton lust.

Missy saw this coupling as a true union of opposites: black and white, male and female, young and old. She wanted it to last forever.

Missy had wrapped herself tightly around him as if to draw him deeper, tighter and closer. He began to move in a driven and intense rhythm, each convulsive shared thrust carrying them to the final, explosive ecstasy.

"I'm coming, Missy."

"Oh, Jackson, give it to me. Come inside me."

Missy was surprised that she had uttered Jackson's name. She did not care. Jason did not seem to care. Perhaps their love-making was releasing some of the inner demons and repressed past memories residing in her sub-conscious.

Jason collapsed against her soft body.

"I can't believe that I've fucked one of the biggest legends in Hollywood."

"It's all in the mind. I can't believe that I have had two earth shattering orgasms in the space of an hour."

They lay in each other's arms until Missy sensed Jason hardening once again.

Jason led her hand to his erection. Half in sleep, her deft hands caressed him. It reminded her of her piano teacher running her fingers over the keyboard, playing scales. They were practised gestures and he allowed her to take control. Once he ejaculated, she withdrew her hand from his penis and he drifted back into a deep slumber.

*** *** *** *** ***

Missy was already up and walking around the bedroom when Jason woke up.

"It is already 7 a.m. Time to get up."

"I like your short robe. Do you have anything underneath?"

"I've just taken a shower and you need to take one too."

"I'm admiring your legs."

Missy looked at her legs.

Jason flicked back his bedsheet, exposing his penis standing at half attention.

"Look what you're doing to me."

Missy looked down at his torso with a smile.

"You've a nice penis but we've other things to do."

"OK. Thanks for last night."

"I needed the love-making badly."

"It was great for me, too."

"No, Jason, you awoke something within me."

"What?"

"For a long time, I was ashamed about my sexual encounters with black men. I tried to repress my sexual urges. Last night taught me that sex with a black man can be liberating. I feel liberated this morning."

"I feel liberated too."

"I've decided to go ahead with the photo shoot. I can't lead two lives. I can't be a hypocrite. I've had black lovers and need to come out of the closet and let everybody know."

"Wow, that's great, Missy. Lisa will be pleased."

Missy put on a mock serious face. "Get up. We're running behind schedule. Take a shower and then bring your car up to the front entrance. We have to leave in thirty minutes."

Jason went into the bathroom. It was still steamy with a mixed waft of feminine perfumes and odours. A comb with blonde hairs caught between the teeth and two crumpled tissues with red lip stick marks had been carelessly left on the wash basin shelf while there was a used shower cap and razor on the edge of the tub. Jason wondered whether Missy had shaved her pussy for the photo shoot.

He took a laundry bag and filled it with Missy's leftovers. They would serve as souvenirs to remind him of this wonderful mid-summer's night.

Chapter 16
Jason – Los Angeles 2006

When Jason parked his car in front of Alexander's studio, he knew that it was time to say good-bye to Missy.

He reached over and kissed her. "Thank you for last night. I will never forget it."

"It was wonderful for me too. You remind me about Jackson and the sex has done wonders for my complexion." It was true. Her face exuded an aura of freshness. She touched her cheek lightly and hopped out of the car.

"Can I see you again?"

"I'm afraid not. I'm flying back to Nashville and I don't think that I should be having a relationship with somebody young enough to be my grandson."

"I've a thing about older woman."

"Why don't you try Lisa? Take my word for it. She likes you. Both of you work together. There are lots of opportunities and she is divorced. Maybe you can liven up her sex life."

"You're giving me ideas."

Jason smiled.

"Now I have to get ready and put on some sexy underwear for the shoot. Young man, your job is to ensure that Alexander does not shoot me from my left side. Also make sure that there are no close-ups under those klieg lights."

They entered Alexander's studio and the receptionist guided them to a dark room where the photos would be shot. Alexander, a good-looking tall man with a pony-tail and an ear ring, was waiting for them and showed Missy the door to her dressing room. "Nancy will make up your face."

While Jason was waiting with Alexander, Lisa came in. She was wearing a smart black office suit with a buttoned jacket and short skirt.

"How is it going?" she asked anxiously.

"Everything is under control and Missy is in the dressing room."

Lisa looked at her watch.

"Does that mean that we can go ahead with the shoot? How did you manage it? I do hope that she was not too difficult?"

"No, she was fine and understanding."

"Good, we'll talk about it later. Where is Richard?"

"Richard will be delayed," replied Alexander. "We'll do some shots of Missy by herself to get warmed up."

Missy came out from her dressing room with her face made up with just a robe over a sexy bra and panty set.

"Okay, where do you want me?"

Alexander was already sweating under the switched-on bright lights.

"Let's take a few shots with your robe to break the ice."

Jason and Lisa watched from a dark corner of the room as Alexander clicked his camera while uttering words of encouragement to Missy.

"How about showing some cleavage?"

Missy lowered her robe from her shoulders and threw her hair back exposing most of her bust.

"Drop the robe and look at me over your shoulder."

Missy did as he ordered and gave him a sexy pout.

"That's perfect, Missy."

"Now I want you over here on the couch. Sit down and raise your legs for me."

Missy pointed her spike heels at the ceiling and held her legs up for him so that the backs of her thighs were framing the camera's view of her face.

Alexander kept on giving instructions, as he clicked on his camera.

"Honey, I don't want you to be nervous. Just try and relax and enjoy yourself. Just go with the flow and you'll be fine."

"Let's go, baby. Take off your bra."

Missy followed his instructions. She sat up, facing the camera. Her breasts were bared, nipples as big as nickel coins.

Alexander moved the tripod closer. "Great, baby! Now show a little tip of the tongue. Hold it."

Jason was fascinated and excited at the same time. He admired how Missy held her stance, her breasts thrust outwards with a look of yearning in her uplifted face. She was a practised professional who followed Alexander's instructions to the letter. This star had certain tangible features – a face, a body, a pair of legs, a voice – but she was capable of assuming personalities ranging from a helpless baby doll to a seductive vamp.

They were still shooting when Jason noticed a black man with a sports bag walk in. He was at least six foot tall, muscular, black as coal and with a clean-shaven head. Alexander called for a break and introduced Richard Collins to everybody. Jason had seen some of Richard's films from the 1970s when he played as a black detective from Harlem. He had retired when the black exploitation films from that era went out of fashion and nobody had heard about him for quite a while. Now he was standing there in flesh-and-blood, an iconic figure like Missy.

Although she only had her panties on, Missy did not seem to be embarrassed in front of the crowd. She sat on the sofa with Lisa while the three men stood around them.

"Rich and I have already worked this out," Missy said. "We've decided on what we'll wear. Alexander, you can start by taking a few shots of us on the sofa and then we'll do a few against the white screen."

Alexander raised his hand. "How about letting me take some shots of both of you in the buff?"

"That wasn't in the contract."

"Don't bother them if it's not in their comfort zone," Lisa interjected.

"I'm okay with being in the nude if it is okay with Missy," said Richard. "We did short nude sequence in the film."

"Rich, those sequences were done from far off with a blurred effect. We've got klieg lights here. I don't think that is a good idea," said Missy. "In any case, there will be no frontal nudity. I don't want the camera to pick up any stretch marks on my stomach."

Missy turned to Jason.

"Can you bring my luggage and hand baggage from your car? My other costume is in my baggage."

Jason picked up the baggage from his car and went straight to Missy's dressing room.

Missy was checking her make-up. Jason stood behind her and admired the mirror image of her large, crystal-blue eyes. He noticed the ageing marks on her neck but the camera could probably overlook them.

She turned around to face him.

"I'm nervous. There's a fine line between interracial erotica and porn. I do hope that Alexander does a tasteful job."

"Alexander is a true professional," Jason reassured her.

Jason noticed that Missy and Richard were a study in contrasts as they came out from their dressing rooms. Missy, in a white transparent negligee, white thong and open toe high heels with silver straps, looked as delicate as a porcelain doll. Richard, huge and muscular, was barefoot with just a pair of black boxers. Jason felt a stirring in his groin.

Jason was struck that Richard had the same skin colour and physical characteristics as Jackson. Did Missy unconsciously reach out into her past by agreeing to pair with Richard?

Alexander gave his instructions. In one shot, he had Missy stretched out on the sofa while Richard hovered over her, looking intently at her. She had her hand under his chin and gazing at him. In another shot, they kept the same position but she was now looking at the camera with her hand on his shoulder. Jason saw that the images were skilfully planned to give the impression that this was foreplay before the act.

Alexander then posed the two in front of a white screen.

Richard stood behind Missy, nibbling her ear with his arms on her sides while she had one white hand against his dark boxers.

"Baby, look at the camera. Give us those bedroom eyes," Alexander pleaded.

Missy obliged with a provocative look.

"Now we need a kissing shot. Give it all you got."

Alexander arranged their postures, showing them where to place their hands.

Jason realised that the photographer knew exactly how to get the best effect. Richard had one arm around Missy's platinum blonde hair and the other on her hip while Missy had one white hand around his neck. Their lips met and they held this posture while Alexander clicked away. It was an artistic composition in black and white.

Jason looked with the fascination of a voyeur with a fetish for interracial sex.

Missy was blonde and he had always considered blondeness is the ultimate sign of whiteness. He had grown up in a culture where blonde women were the prized possessions of white men, the most desired of women but denied to black men. Yet, Richard, black as coal, was holding Missy, so pale and white, in his arms. Just fifty years ago, he could have been lynched for just leering at a white woman. Both were performers posing for the camera but the image conveyed the secret and forbidden sexual desire of a black man and a white woman for each other.

Jason felt a slight stab of jealousy. Last night he had possessed this woman and loved her in her vulnerable state. Today she had resumed her role of a blonde Venus, eluding him, and he had returned to worshipping her like the thousands of her admirers.

"Let's take one shot with both of you in the buff," said Alexander. Missy looked uncertainly at Richard. He smiled. "Why not give it a try?"

Without much ado, Richard dropped his boxers. Jason could not help but examine his sexual parts. His phallus, flaccid and covered with a thick foreskin, hung way below his pendulous testicles. Jason thought that he did not seem to be embarrassed to be buck black naked in front of two white women.

It was now Missy's turn. She took off her negligee and untied her thong to reveal a body with fairly full breasts and just a little rounding at the stomach. Jason noticed that her pussy was bare and remembered that she had shaved off her light flaxen strands of pubic hair. There was a barely visible slit within a deliciously white vulva and it gave the effect of a mature woman with a girlish pussy.

"Please, Alexander, there will be no frontal shots," Missy pleaded.

"No," replied Alexander. "I just want of you to take the same pose as before, kissing each other."

Missy and Richard embraced each other. Alexander took several side shots, repeating enthusiastically, "This is sheer poetry in black and white."

When they came apart from their hug, Jason noticed that Richard's penis was semi-erect. He did not seem to be concerned.

"Christ, Rich, you've leaked your pre-cum all over my stomach," Missy said. "Does anybody have a paper napkin?"

Richard smiled. "I'm sorry but I couldn't control myself. Look what you've done to me." He pointed to his penis, leaned forward and gave Missy a light peck on her lips.

Lisa came forward with a couple of paper napkins and Missy took a tissue to dry the wet area around her lower abdomen. Jason saw something erotic even in this small gesture, as he imagined Richard's black penis leaking pre-cum while pressed against Missy's white stomach.

The two performers left to get dressed while Lisa and Jason moved to the receptionist's room.

"That went off well," Lisa exclaimed. "Jason thanks for helping out. Please help Missy pack her stuff in the limousine." She picked up her cell phone to instruct the limousine to drive in front of Alexander's studio.

Jason felt his erection subsiding but his boxer pants were uncomfortably sticky. He had seen quite a show.

When Missy returned, fully dressed, Lisa held a farewell meeting before she left.

"I can't thank Jason enough," Missy told Lisa. "He released the inner demons within me and, this morning, I was relaxed for the shoot."

"I am glad that it worked out well," Lisa said, casting a meaningful look at Jason.

They talked for a while about some future projects. Jason assumed that it had to do with another interracial feature.

"Jake will get in touch with you," Missy said. "I want Jason to handle the public relations part."

"I will be discussing this with Jason," Lisa replied.

When the time came to part, Missy planted a wet kiss on Jason's cheek. "Thanks for last night," she whispered.

Jason knew that his attitude towards sex with white women had changed forever. The best sex with a white woman was when emotions and lust combined to give a sensual high. Missy had given him a lesson that he would not forget.

Chapter 17
Lisa – 2006

"Can you drop me at the office?"

Lisa turned to Jason after they saw off Missy.

"Sure, it's on my way."

"I'd given my car for servicing and they've delivered it to the office."

"How did you come to the studio?"

"I had a limo drop me here but let it go since I didn't know how long the shoot would last."

Lisa knew that she could have easily ordered another limousine to drop her home but she wanted to spend some time with Jason.

"No problem, if you don't mind my rundown Hyundai."

They got into his car and he started driving towards the freeway.

"What are your plans for today?"

"I've got nothing lined up."

"How would you like to drive me to my cottage in Newport Beach?"

"I haven't been that side for a while. That will be a nice change."

Lisa explained that she had just remembered that her neighbour was organising a yard sale and she wanted to get rid of some the stuff that had piled up at her weekend retreat.

"I also need to clean out my garage. Maybe you can help out."

"I'd be glad to be of assistance, Ms Donovan."

"You can call me Lisa when we're alone."

"Thanks, Lisa."

Jason sensed that he was in for another episode.

you seem to be game for anything. You never say no."

"I'm grateful for the chance you've given me to work with Missy."

Lisa looked closely at Jason.

"You spent the night with Missy?" Lisa made the question sound like a statement.

"Well, yes. It wasn't planned that way. It just happened. Missy didn't mind. I'd gone up to handle some work and then stayed on."

"Is that why you're still wearing last night's tuxedo?"

"Yeah, I drove straight from her hotel to Alexander's place."

Lisa was happy that Jason told the truth. She had suspected something since Missy had been vague about what took place after dinner.

"Whatever happened last night is not my business. I had told you to make sure that she made it to the studio this morning and you made it happen."

Lisa was sure that Missy must have seduced the young man. She was a real cradle snatcher. Jason was young enough to be her grandson.

Lisa's indignation gave way to envy when she speculated about Missy's sex life. Some Hollywood stars had insatiable sexual appetites. They would sleep with anything that moved.

"What did Missy tell you?"

Lisa saw that Jason was concerned.

"Missy praised you. She feels that you are a conscientious employee."

Jason looked pleased.

"She was also quite taken up by you. We made some plans that concerned you."

"Can we talk about it?"

"Missy said that she wanted you to handle her public relations."

"Wow. She really said that?"

"Well, she felt that you understood her viewpoint regarding the interracial issues involved in this film."

"Missy is a great actress and very easy to get along with. I'd love to handle her PR."

"You'll report directly to me on this assignment. It'll be easier for both of us to work directly with Missy."

"You mean John will not be in on this deal?"

"Missy and I discussed a new project for you, which you'll manage on your own.."

"Is this for real?"

Lisa saw Jason look sideways at her.

"If Missy's film is a success, she feels that there could be a market for interracial romance films done in a tasteful manner. Hollywood is not yet ready but there are a few independent producers willing to put up some money."

"How do we fit in?"

"We'll need to sign up senior actors willing to perform in mainstream interracial features. This will help us in working out a deal with a producer for a film or even a TV series. Do you think that you could handle this project and sign up black actors?"

"Lisa, I really don't know but I can give it a shot. Maybe Missy would be willing to do a second segment."

"Yes, Jason, that's a good thought. Missy is a true professional. The shots of Richard and her in the buff were tastefully done but highly erotic."

Lisa felt a tinge between her legs when she thought about the interracial photo shoot. She had been turned on by the visual images of the lily white blonde and coal black stud posing in the nude. Richard's penis proved that some of the stories she heard about black men were true.

"We can probably work with the same team that did the first feature. Lisa, let me think about it and come back to you with a proposal for an interracial erotic features. Of-course we'll to also think about promotion of DVDs and video on demand. I am really excited."

"Hold your horses, young man. Let's see how this feature plays out in the market."

"The photo shoot got me excited and I'm sure that the publicity shots will make the feature a success."

Jason's enthusiasm was infectious. Lisa felt that their instincts were right.

"I'm optimistic too. Missy and Richard made a very sexy couple. The publicity stills will do wonders for the film. I'm glad that we're not going to the office because we can discuss this a little more in detail."

Lisa listened to Jason's ideas. She was impressed by his knowledge of social media and how it could be used to create hype for the film. The young man certainly had a fresh approach. The company could use somebody who could think outside the box.

"Can you work out a PR budget that we can present to the studio?"

"I'll work on it the first thing on Monday morning."

Jason took the highway exit for Newport Beach and followed Lisa's instructions to get to her place.

"My mind is already clicking. I know a couple of retired basketball players who would be happy to recycle themselves as actors."

"That's not a bad idea."

Lisa thought about Wilt Chamberlain who claimed that he had slept with twenty thousand women. There was also Dennis Rodman who had had an affair with Madonna. Black basketball players did symbolise male virility. The image of black basketball players embracing creamy white burlesque stars sent a thrill through her body.

"I'm sure that there are also a couple of older white porn stars who would like to do a feature with some real acting."

Lisa wondered whether Jason was into interracial porn. There was also so much available on the Internet. May be he already knew names of white actresses who had featured with black males in adult films.

She also speculated on Missy's opinion that Jason had a hankering for older white women.

She felt that Jason was the right choice for the new project. Perhaps that had something to do with her impulsive decision to invite him to her weekend cottage.

"I like working for you, Lisa, and think the world about you."

"Jason, you're a silly boy." Her hand touched his shoulder lightly. "Hey, we're almost there. Welcome to my private world."

Lisa instructed Jason to turn into an estate and used a remote control in her key chain to automatically open the garage door. Jason parked the Hyundai in a garage packed with odd items ranging from bundles of clothes to kitchen appliances.

"I want to get rid of all these things to clear out the house. You can help yourself to anything you want."

"Do you want me to clear this stuff?"

"My neighbour is having a yard sale this weekend and I need your help to carry some of my surplus things over to his place. It'll take less than half an hour."

"No problem, Lisa."

A door led to the kitchen and Jason followed Lisa to the drawing room.

"Do we start now?"

"First you'll need to open all the windows before I look for some sensible clothes."

While Jason was opening the windows, Lisa moved from the drawing room into the bedroom. She shucked off her high heels, took off her jacket and dropped her skirt to the floor. Moving around in a short slip, she opened a chest of drawers and started searching.

Lisa was surprised when she heard Jason's footsteps.

"I'm sorry."

Jason looked visibly embarrassed. Lisa's initial irritation eased when she saw his contrite expression.

"I was getting into something comfortable. You can draw the curtains back and open the two windows here."

Lisa noticed that Jason was still staring at her. She sensed that this young black was aroused but not in any threatening way. Feeling exposed, she decided to defuse the situation with some innocent banter.

"I usually strip down to shorts when I'm here."

"Good idea."

Lisa heard the sound of window latches being opened. He was busy elsewhere.

She found a pair of shorts and quickly pulled them up under her slip. Next she drew her slip up over her head.

"The windows are open."

She turned around, dressed in her brassiere and shorts. Instinctively her hands shot up to cover her breasts.

"Oh, I'm still changing."

She noticed Jason's smirk. His eyes had taken on a lustful look. It frightened her. They were alone in her bedroom. She had heard stories of black men raping white women.

"Don't worry about me, Lisa." Jason stayed at his corner, watching her

Lisa turned around to look in the open drawer. She found a blouse and put it on.

"I have to get out of this tuxedo. Do you have a spare pair of jeans?"

Although Jason's request appeared to be reasonable, Lisa resented the demanding tone of his voice.

"I don't know. Perhaps my ex left a pair of jeans somewhere."

Lisa moved to a cupboard. From the corner of her eye, she observed Jason taking off his coat and laying it on her bed.

"You can try this pair."

Jason moved towards her and took a well-worn pair of jeans. He examined them.

"Your ex was a big man too."

Lisa just nodded. She did not want to get into any discussion about her ex-husband.

"They might fit me."

Jason took off his trousers. Lisa saw that he had an erection, his penis acting like a tent pole beneath his boxer shorts.

Although Lisa was momentarily aroused, she was upset at what she perceived as Jason's impertinence. She felt that she must take control over the situation.

"Jason, would you mind changing in the bathroom? Please behave yourself. Stop this display at once."

Jason's demeanour changed immediately.

"I'm sorry. Lisa, I didn't mean to offend you."

He moved to the bathroom with the jeans.

Lisa was relieved that Jason had reverted to his earlier polite behaviour. For a moment she had felt as if she had been caged with a lustful black man. The thought excited her and frightened her at the same time. It had been a close shave.

Jason came out, barefoot, dressed in a pair of jeans that were a bit short. He was holding his trousers in one hand and the shoes in the other.

"You can put your stuff in the garage. There are also a couple of sneakers there."

Lisa wanted to get both of them out of her bedroom.

When they were in the drawing room, Lisa decided to set the rules.

"I was not pleased with your behaviour in the bedroom. Do you always make it a habit to undress in front of women?"

"Lisa, please excuse me."

Jason seemed truly apologetic. Lisa was surprised at the sudden shift. She was not racist but surmised that he had reverted to the role of house nigger from plantation stud.

"Jason, let's get one thing straight. I brought you to my place because I thought that we could talk about your place in the new project and I figured that you could help me with moving some stuff. I'm shocked at your conduct and I'm not pleased at all."

"This will not happen again." Jason looked down on the floor.

"I do hope so. Remember, I run the company and I do not indulge in any type of improper relationships with subordinates. Besides do you think that I'll become your white mistress so that you can brag about it to your friends?"

"Believe me, Lisa, I respect you too much to ever even think about doing something like that," Jason protested.

"Alright let's forget that this ever happened. Let's go to the garage to look for a pair of exercise shoes."

Lisa saw that Jason looked truly repentant. She hoped that their professional relationship had not been affected. She just wanted him to know that she was his boss. It had nothing to do with race but she needed to keep her distance from this man.

For the next hour, Lisa observed that Jason assuming the role of an obedient employee eager to please his employer.

Jason's job was to move a number of surplus items from the garage to Lisa's neighbour's place where the yard sale would begin the next day. He moved the heavy items first: an old lawn mower, a mountain bike, an inflatable raft and a vacuum cleaner. There were also many kitchen utensils, crockery and cutlery.

Lisa was in a better mood after Jason had laid out everything in the neighbour's garden. This spring cleaning was overdue and the garage sale was a good opportunity. She had priced most of the items at just a dollar.

Now Lisa felt that she had to make it up to Jason.

"Are you in a hurry to return to Los Angeles?" she asked. "If not, we could walk to the beach to watch the sunset. I will buy you a drink."

They walked but both were quiet.

Lisa pictured them as a black panther and a white snow leopard warily sizing up each other, waiting for the other to make the first move.

Lisa stopped at a beachside café.

"This is a nice place to see the sun set."

They took a table with a clear view of the sea.

Lisa observed Jason when the waitress, a pretty blonde in a short skirt, came to take their order. He still seemed subdued.

"I'll have a vodka martini. What about you?"

"I'll have just a can of Coke."

They sat for a while contemplating the view until Lisa finally broke their silence. "I'm sorry about my outburst this morning. I guess that I overreacted."

Jason just nodded.

"It had to do with some bad experiences during my time at Berkeley."

"Was it with black men?"

"More than once, I had a black guy walk past me, whispering 'Can I fuck you?' Many of these young black men had no respect for white women."

"I know what you're saying. May be it is the black man's way of getting back at whitey."

"Propositioning a woman on the street? I think that many black men see white women are easy conquests."

"It's got to do with race. We blacks are conditioned. We're living in a white society. Some black men see white women as something exotic."

"To be truthful, there was a time when I became afraid of black men. When I saw you this morning looking at me, I was reminded me of my college days."

"I meant no disrespect."

"You were taking off your trousers with an erection in your boxer shorts. There was no need for this kind of exhibitionism."

"I just got excited when I saw you in a brassiere."

"Haven't you ever seen any other woman in a brassiere?"

"Sure and I have seen lots of women in bikinis on the beach. We just happened to be in your bedroom."

"You barged in while I was changing."

"That was not my intention."

Lisa looked at Jason. She smiled.

"You're a poor liar."

Jason smiled shamefacedly.

"Perhaps I was hard on you but I like to keep my distance from men. I've put in a lot of work in my agency and it's not always been easy to be accepted as a woman CEO. There have been times when I had to plead with our banker to be able to meet the payroll for the month."

"Gee, I didn't realize that the going could be so hard."

"It became especially hard when Hank, my ex-husband, left the business."

"Did both of you start the agency?"

"Yes, Hank got the clients while I handled the PR work."

"Why did you split?"

"Hank found another woman. She was young and rich. They decided to go on a round the world trip in her sailboat."

"That must have been hard."

"It hurt my self-esteem and I threw myself into my work."

"You can always find another man. It'll make life easier for you."

"At fifty-five, it is difficult to find a suitable man who could fit in my professional life. Look at me. I'm already grey-haired."

"If you don't mind me saying so you look ten years younger. I think that you can still find a man if you tried."

"Jason, you're just being nice. Let's watch the sun set and then go back."

They watched the sun set, a red ball sinking over the horizon. Nobody said a word.

When they reached Lisa's place, it was way past twilight.

"We've been perspiring quite a bit. I need to shower. Why don't you also shower in the guest bedroom?"

Lisa showed Jason the guest bedroom with its attached bathroom.

She then took a hot shower in her bathroom, leaving the bathroom mirror completely steamed.

Wrapping herself in a bathing robe, Lisa looked at herself in the dressing room mirror. She applied a little make-up and generously doused her neck and shoulders with Chanel No 5.

Lisa saw Jason was surprised when he saw her enter the guest bedroom. He was sprawled on the bed with a towel wrapped around his torso.

"Hi, now it's my turn to barge into your bedroom."

Jason sat up, adjusting his towel around himself. He smiled.
"That makes us quits."

Lisa sat on the other side of the bed.

"I'm going to lie down on. It's more comfortable."

Lisa stretched out on the bed. She saw Jason also do the same. Both were lying on their backs, side by side, looking at the ceiling.

"The shower has done wonders for me."

"I feel good too."

"I also feel good that we've been able to talk frankly."

"I also think so, Lisa."

"By the way, I'm still curious about Missy. You must have had an interesting talk last night."

"Yes. She told me a few things about her past that made me understand her motives for doing an interracial feature."

Lisa became curious. She wanted to know more about this aspect of Missy's life.

"Can you share your input with me? It will help me to work with Missy."

Lisa listened as Jason told her about his research on Missy and how he happened to stumble upon her relationship with Jackson Coots.

"It would have been pure dynamite in those days if it was known that a Hollywood star was having a relationship with a black prize fighter."

"The studio broke up the affair. They just had too much money invested in Missy's career."

"I must admire Missy. She had guts. She has really lived a full life."

"What about you, Lisa? Don't you think of sharing your life with a partner?"

Lisa thought about her own life. After her divorce, she had avoided any emotional relationships. She did not want to get hurt.

"I've been too busy lately and have yet to meet the right man. Most of the good men I know are married."

"You work too hard. May be you should make some time available to make new friends."

Lisa realized that she even kept a distance with her employees. May be she should invite Linda and John for a meal at her place.

May be she needed to mix more and be open minded about making new friends socially.

"What about you, Jason? Are you going steady with somebody?"

"Well, not exactly but it is difficult to explain."

"I don't get you, Jason."

"I prefer to play the field."

"It seems understandable for a handsome young man like you. I imagine that you must have already broken quite a few hearts."

"I did have a relationship with a cheerleader in college but we haven't seen each other for a while. The job has been keeping me busy."

"You must be missing her."

"There was a problem. She was white and her family didn't approve."

"That's a pity."

"No. I don't think it wouldn't have worked out any way."

"Why?"

"She was too immature. When I come to think about it, I prefer older women."

"You're going through a phase of youthful fantasies. Eventually you'll find somebody closer to your age."

"I am looking for women of class. You're very classy. You are beautiful. You're my kind of woman."

Lisa felt flattered that a twenty-two-year-old man thought that she was appealing. She wondered whether it had to do with a fetish for mature woman or a black male's lust for white women. Perhaps it was a bit of both.

"You seem to prefer white women."

"I've known some nice black girls but I've had great relations with white girls."

"Is it only about sex?"

"No, but it is part of the package. I'm just more comfortable with white women."

Lisa had heard rumours about how black men loved to have sex with white women. She wondered whether Jason knew what to do or if he would be an immature lover.

"What's so special about white women?"

""I guess we black men have been conditioned by the white world around us. White women set the standard for female beauty. You know blondes with blue eyes and that kind of stuff. As a boy I used to fantasize about Nicole Kidman."

"I bet you made your fantasies come true with Missy."

Jason grinned.

"I'm not telling."

Lisa laughed. She found Jason's discretion to be endearing. At the same time, she was gushing between her legs. She felt like a teen-ager. Still, she had reservations.

"Missy showed me that the beautiful side of interracial sex. She has never been afraid to show her emotions. I don't know if I could do the same."

"You think too much."

"I guess that comes with my age."

"For me, you are a vibrant and sexy woman."

Lisa heard the mattress squish as Jason leaned on his arm and moved sideways to face her.

"Rubbish, Jason. You're just being nice. I bet you tried the same approach with Missy."

Lisa moved up and rested her back against the head of the bed. Her bathrobe opened. She left her cleavage exposed, pretending not to notice Jason's gaze at her chest.

"No, Lisa. This is different. I've always had the hots for you. Don't you have the same urge? We can have sex and nobody will know. I promise."

Lisa was surprised at Jason's direct approach. She had to decide. It was now or never.

"That's quite a proposition." She smiled.

"I mean it."

"Well, ever since Hank left, my sex life hasn't been much."

"Let's do something about it."

Jason leaned over and kissed her. It was a chaste kiss. Lisa took in his odour – a combination of musk and Ivory soap.

"I normally don't get intimate with young men because they tend to blabber. Promise me that nobody in the office will ever know about it."

"I promise."

Jason kissed her again, probing his tongue in her mouth. She was surprised at his kissing skills. The young man obviously had had a great deal of practice.

"My, that was quite a kiss."

Lisa gasped for breath.

"One more, please."

Jason kissed her hungrily and opened her bath robe to expose her breasts. He thrust his tongue into her mouth again while flicking his fingers lightly over a nipple.

"I want to kiss your tits."

Lisa cupped Jason's head while he ran his tongue over one of her nipples and then sucked on it.

Jason stopped for a breather. "You've got great tits. I could suck them forever."

Lisa's mind flipped between conflicting emotions. She was in bed with a young employee. It had been a long time since somebody had fondled her. She needed this. Jason was so eager. What could be the harm?

"You're a sweet little boy. I feel so old."

"You look great to me."

Lisa hoped that Jason had not noticed the sag in her breasts when he started sucking on her other nipple.

"Lisa, I want to taste your pussy."

Jason moved downwards, brushing his lips over her stomach.

"I'm not sure whether I'm ready for this."

Lisa could not remember the last time when a man had gone down on her. She was relieved that she had recently trimmed her bush but now hoped that the few stray grey hairs were not too prominent.

"I'm glad that you haven't shaved."

"Why? I thought you young men prefer girls to shave nowadays."

"Most girls do but I don't care."

"Even older women shave. Missy was bald at the photo shoot this morning."

"It works for blondes like Missy but sometimes I like to see a little hair below."

Jason ran his fingers back and forth across her vulva lips.

"You've a beautiful pussy with such fine pink lips."

Lisa was moist. She was glad that she had showered and did not have to worry about any odours. Jason was separating her lips and she raised her pelvis at his touch.

"You've even got a cute clit."

Lisa felt Jason moving his tongue over the nub of her barely visible clitoris and then up and down her vulva lips. She moaned and clamped his head between his thighs.

Jason rose to look up on her. "This is prime pussy with a pink tuna flavour. I could eat you for breakfast, lunch and dinner."

"You're too much."

Jason rose up to kiss her again. Lisa tasted herself on his lips, finding it to have a slightly brackish flavour.

Lisa dropped her reserve and kissed Jason back with fervour. They continued kissing for quite a while.

"I think that I'm going to follow Missy's example. Take off your robe. I want to see what I missed this morning."

Jason hesitated for a minute. He took off his bath robe to expose his penis. It stood up like a curved scimitar.

"I'm sorry but I'm all excited again. You do this to me."

"We must do something about it. Lie down on the bed."

Lisa opened a night table drawer, picked a small packet and opened it. The condom dated back to the time when she had been with Mark.

Jason watched as she expertly rolled it down over his penis and then slowly stroked it.

"You've a magnificent penis:"

"I've got a black stud who thinks I'm sexy and I'm going to let him fuck me."

Lisa felt so desirable that she was getting wetter by the minute.

"I can't wait to be inside you."

Lisa released Jason and he positioned himself over her. Edging forward, he pushed his penis toward her moist entrance.

"I haven't had sex for quite a while and you're big."

Lisa looked down as Jason crawled over her.

"I'll be gentle," he said in a reassuring tone.

Lisa gasped as he slowly eased the tip of his shaft into her. She spread her legs wider.

"It's okay. I'll be fine," she whispered.

Lisa felt Jason slip in deeper and stretch her in enjoyable ways.

"It feels good inside you."

She felt Jason letting himself down onto her and loved the feeling of his muscular body on top of hers.

"It is good for me also," she said breathlessly.

Jason moved in slow strokes, pressing deeper each time.

"I'm in all the way but you're tight."

Lisa pulled Jason closer, as he began to stroke harder.

"Oh, this feels good."

Lisa felt Jason kiss her neck and suck on her ear lobe. He put his hands under her hips and started pounding her. She raised her hips and moved against him in the same rhythm.

"Don't mind me," Lisa moaned. She thrust her hips against him, experiencing a powerful orgasm. Almost immediately, she felt another one throbbing between her legs and then another one. She had never experienced such multiple orgasms before.

For several minutes she clung to him, eyes closed, her vagina still throbbing from her sexual high.

"Are you alright?" Jason looked worried.

Lisa opened her eyes.

"I came. Now it's your turn."

She saw Jason's expression change to one of concentration, as he started pounding her again.

"Let me feel you come, babe."

Lisa was surprised that the last word had slipped out of her mouth. Had it to do with their age difference?

She felt him throb inside her. Both quivered and held each other tight.

They lay quietly, their hearts beating almost in unison against each other.

Jason exclaimed, "Wow."

"If you've nothing planned, let's spend the weekend here," Lisa suggested. "I've some catching up to do as far as my sexual life is concerned.

Jason kissed her tenderly. "I'm your black slave. Your wishes are my commands."

"I'll be your white mistress but it'll be just for this weekend."

"I agree."

"On Monday, I'll revert to being your employer."

"I'll always respect you."

"This weekend will never repeat again."

Lisa saw Jason nod with a look of sad resignation.

"What you're saying is that this will only be a memory for both of us."

"Well, you know the consequences if it ever comes out that we had an affair?"

"Yes, I understand. We played out our fantasies about black and white sex and now it's over."

Lisa stroked Jason's cheek.

"It goes beyond you being a young black man and me being a mature white woman. I'm also your employer. Be reasonable."

"Yes, I understand. I'll never do anything to embarrass you, Lisa."

Lisa was relieved that she could count on Jason to be discrete. She put on her bath robe and got up.

"Hey, where are you going?"

"I'm going to see what we have in the fridge for a quick bite. Stay where you are."

"Are you coming back soon?"

Lisa saw that Jason was hardening.

"How can you? We just had sex."

"That's what a twenty-two-year old male is all about. Our hormones are on over-drive."

Lisa made up her mind that she would catch up on this weekend to make up for all that she had missed over the past years.

Chapter 18
Jason – 2006

Jason had had an eventful and productive morning.

Lisa had called for a meeting with Linda and John when she announced that Jason's assignment to Project Rainbow. He would be directly reporting to her.

Jason was surprised when John readily agreed to Linda's proposals. John added that Jason was best suited to handle Missy's public relations connected with the launch of her new feature. He also welcomed the concept of the agency working with independent studios in promoting interracial romance features. It was a niche market that could develop in the coming years.

Jason could not believe what he was hearing. He had always imagined John to be a racist who could not tolerate the idea of black men making it with white women. May be John was open-minded when it came to making a buck from softcore interracial porn.

After the meeting, Jason was a state of exhilaration but felt physically totally drained. Sunday had been spent in bed with Lisa. They had been insatiable in their sexual desires. Jason's penis felt sore. He was sure that Lisa was sore too. It would take a few days for him to recover from the excesses of this past memorable weekend.

"Jason."

Jason was startled in his reverie. Looking up, he saw Linda standing over his desk. She was smiling.

"You seem to have made a big impression on Lisa last Friday."

"I don't know what you mean."

Jason tried to look innocent. He knew that Linda had no inkling about his weekend with Lisa.

"Well, it's been rather sudden. Lisa hardly knew you and now she is putting you on a new project." Linda looked at him with an air of suspicion.

"This has been a surprise for me also."

"I'll be putting up an announcement on the notice board as soon as Lisa sends me the text."

"Thanks."

"Congratulations and best of luck."

Linda turned away.

Jason felt good. He decided to drop by Annabelle's desk.

"How's the going?"

Annabelle was engrossed a stack of papers. She looked up.

"I'm busy on the Harry Stern contract. There are a couple of things that I need to understand."

"Do you need any help?"

"No thanks. I will discuss it with John."

Jason was secretly relieved that his offer of help had been refused. He had other things to do. Annabelle had always been cordial but cool with him. He needed to be with people with warmth.

Jason thought about Gina. She was at the basketball game last weekend and could give him an update.

Gina was busy sorting mail.

"How is our basketball hero doing today?"

Jason was amused that Gina always greeted him in the same way. Maybe it was her way of marking their common interest in the sport.

"How did LBSU do on Saturday?"

Gina described the highlights of the game.

While she was talking, Jason observed her face. She could be pretty if she lost a few pounds. He promised himself to take her out for a game and also get her a membership when he joins a health club. She definitely had potential.

After she finished, she looked at him questioningly.

"There are rumours in the office."

"What are you hearing?"

"You're being reassigned to another job."

"Yes, that's true. Wait for the announcement on the notice board."

"Are you okay with the change?"

Jason saw that Gina looked anxious.

"Yes. It's a new challenge but I think that I'll manage."

"You can count on me for any support that you might need."

Gina looked as if she meant it and Jason knew that he could count on her.

"I know. I might need your help in making contacts with retired basketball players."

Gina looked puzzled.

"Why? You also know quite a few players yourself."

Jason smiled.

"You've an encyclopaedic memory about basketball history. I'll tell you about it later."

Jason decided that Julie would work with him on the new project. Black men could relate to this white girl.

On the way back to his desk, Harriet called out to him.

"Jason, please prepare your expense voucher for your car expenses. Lisa told me to remind you."

"Thanks, Harriet. I will do so by this afternoon."

Harriet nodded understandingly.

People seemed friendlier and things were going to work out fine in this office.

Epilogue
Jason – 2011

Jason clicked on the attachment that came with Lisa's e-mail.

It was a newspaper clipping scan with Missy's photo. The text mentioned that Melissa 'Missy' McGuire had been awarded the Governor's Prize for promoting race relations in the state of Tennessee.

"She deserved it," Jason said under his breath.

He picked up his cell phone.

"Hello, Gina. Did you see the clipping about Missy?"

He heard her response.

"I'm preparing a PR release for the press. Missy's third interracial romance feature had also been a great hit. This release will be the icing on the cake."

"By the way, how is the shoot going?"

They talked for a while before Jason clicked the red button on his phone.

Jason thought that it had been a smart move to move Gina from the mailroom to the Rainbow project. Thanks to her contacts in the basketball world, she had been able to recruit quite a few senior black players to act in interracial features with white stars. The idea of combining sports personalities with Hollywood stars had worked well.

Gina was now on location, supervising the shooting of a new feature but she would be back soon.

He had been dating Gina and also going to the gym with her. Over the past years she had lost thirty pounds and looked really pretty now. Their sex sessions were also great. Life could not get any better.

*** *** *** *** *** ***

Acknowledgements

I want to thank Presley St-Claire, who consented to the use of a still photo from one of her video clips for the book cover. In case you want to access Presley St-Claire's web site, please click on this link:

http://www.southern-charms.com/presleystclaire/main.htm

You can follow Presley at:

@PresleyStClaire

About the Author

Nick Shaw writes about interracial sex between consulting adults. The common theme in all his books is the forbidden aspect that makes sexual relations so exciting for the two consenting partners, namely a white woman and a black man.

If you are a member of 'Kindle Unlimited', you can download my e-books for free.

Other books by Nick Shaw

Nick Shaw's interracial sex books include:

"Joshua's Awakening – A young African's Encounters with mature English women": A young immigrant in the English city of Newcastle meets white women with different racial attitudes towards blacks.

Kindle e-book link:
https://www.amazon.com/Joshuas-Awakening-Africans-Encounters-Englishwomen-ebook/dp/B01JDLH6B2/ref=sr_1_1?s=digital-text&ie=UTF8&qid=1469973178&sr=1-1&keywords=Joshua%27s+Awakening#navbar

Print book link:
https://www.amazon.com/Joshuas-Awakening-Africans-Encounters-Englishwomen-ebook/dp/B01JDLH6B2/ref=sr_1_2?s=books&ie=UTF8&qid=1497624017&sr=1-2&keywords=Joshua%27s+Awakening

Nick Shaw's 'In Praise of White Women' series include the following books:

"The Enigmatic English Escort": A coloured man meets the divorced wife of an ex-colleague only to discover that she has started working as an escort. He becomes her best client and falls in love with her. What does the future hold for them?

Kindle e-book link:
https://www.amazon.com/dp/B01M6XPFZ8/ref=sr_1_1?s=digital-text&ie=UTF8&qid=1476678551&sr=1-1&keywords=The+Enigmatic+English+Escort+Nick+Shaw

Print book link:
https://www.amazon.com/Enigmatic-English-Escort-Praise-White/dp/1520974868/ref=sr_1_1?s=books&ie=UTF8&qid=1492588744&sr=1-1&keywords=The+Enigmatic+English+Escort

"Encounters with Streetwalkers and Escorts":
Stories of meetings with women of easy virtue over a span of five decades.

Kindle e-book link:
https://www.amazon.com/Encounters-Streetwalkers-Escorts-Praise-White-ebook/dp/B071F8DJ2W/ref=sr_1_1?s=digital-text&ie=UTF8&qid=1497625081&sr=1-1&keywords=Encounters+with+Streetwalkers+and+Escorts
Print version link:
https://www.amazon.com/Encounters-Streetwalkers-Escorts-Praise-White/dp/152150279X/ref=sr_1_1?s=books&ie=UTF8&qid=1497625026&sr=1-1&keywords=Encounters+with+Streetwalkers+and+Escorts

The books in the 'Bermuda Cruise Encounters' series include:

"Diane's Story – Bermuda Cruise Encounters": A fiftyish white widow on a cruise to Bermuda has a romance with an eighteen-year coloured cabin boy.

Kindle e-book link:
https://www.amazon.com/Dianes-Story-Bermuda-Cruise-Encounters-ebook/dp/B01N1P3W29/ref=sr_1_1?ie=UTF8&qid=1489218700&sr=8-1&keywords=diane%27s+story+bermuda+cruise+encounters

119

Print book link:
https://www.amazon.com/Dianes-Story-Bermuda-Cruise-Encounters/dp/152108792X/ref=sr_1_1?s=books&ie=UTF8&qid=1497624542&sr=1-1&keywords=diane%27s+story+bermuda+cruise+encounters

"Tina's Story – Bermuda Cruise Encounters": A white porn star goes on a cruise to Bermuda to perform in an interracial feature with a local black escort.

Kindle e-book link:
https://www.amazon.com/Tinas-Story-Bermuda-Cruise-Encounters-ebook/dp/B06XKK9CBJ/ref=sr_1_1?s=digital-text&ie=UTF8&qid=1490540656&sr=1-1&keywords=tina%27s+story+bermuda+cruise+encounters

Print book link:
https://www.amazon.com/Tinas-Story-Bermuda-Cruise-Encounters-ebook/dp/B06XKK9CBJ/ref=sr_1_1?s=books&ie=UTF8&qid=1497624746&sr=1-1&keywords=Tina%27s+Story+Bermuda+Cruise+Encounters

Connect with Nick Shaw

I appreciate you for taking the time to read my book.

If you are a member of 'Kindle Unlimited', all my e-books can be downloaded for free.

Please you have any comments or suggestions, please send me an e-mail at:

    yxc4u@hotmail.com

You can also follow me on Twitter:

    @ShawAuthor

I would be grateful if you could post a review even if it is not very favourable. We independent authors need reviews. Your review can help another reader take a decision on whether to read the book or not.

Printed in Great Britain
by Amazon